Puffin Books

BAGTHORPES HAUNTED

Their holiday house is supposed to be haunted, and, so determined is Mr Bagthorpe to see a ghost, he's even conducted a seance to try and produce one. Now he wants to find the Mr Jones who has rented them the house. But which Mr Jones is he? Rosie discovers there are 36,750 Jones's in the telephone book and calculates that it will cost Mr Bagthorpe £3,750 to ring them all from the phone box to locate *his* Mr Jones.

Meanwhile, Daisy Parker and her Billy Goat Gruff are wreaking havoc wherever they go, terrorizing the villagers and greatly adding to the Bagthorpes' by now almost legendary reputation in the neighbourhood. Mrs Fosdyke takes refuge in The Welsh Harp and is soon maligning the Bagthorpes, much to the delight of the locals.

When Mrs Bagthorpe organizes an expedition to an auction to buy some basic items of furniture, like a draining board for Mrs Fosdyke and a desk for her husband, Mr Bagthorpe rather unexpectedly acquires much more than they had intended – including the biggest wardrobe anyone has ever seen! And Grandma purchases an ancient gramophone and some extremely battered opera recordings which she inflicts on the household at a nerve-wracking volume in the interests of educating them all.

As disaster is added to calamity, so tolerance is stretched to breaking point and desperate measures are required to produce the ghosts that Mr Bagthorpe is determined to see before he will allow the family to return home.

Helen Cresswell was born in Nottinghamshire and was educated there and at Kings College, London. She now lives in an old farmhouse in Robin Hood country with her family. Of the more than forty books she has written, some have been televised and four were runners-up for the Carnegie Medal.

D1369099

Other books by Helen Cresswell

ABSOLUTE ZERO
BAGTHORPES ABROAD
BAGTHORPES UNLIMITED
BAGTHORPES v. THE WORLD
THE BEACHCOMBERS
THE BONGLEWEED
DEAR SHRINK
A GIFT FROM WINKLESEA
LIZZIE DRIPPING
THE NIGHT-WATCHMEN
ORDINARY JACK
THE PIEMAKERS
THE SECRET WORLD OF POLLY FLINT

Helen Cresswell

Bagthorpes Haunted

being the sixth part of the
Bagthorpe Saga

Illustrated by Jill Bennett

Puffin Books
in association with Faber and Faber

Puffin Books, Penguin Books Ltd, Harmondsworth, Middlesex, England
Viking Penguin Inc., 40 West 23rd Street, New York, New York 10010, U.S.A.
Penguin Books Australia Ltd, Ringwood, Victoria, Australia
Penguin Books Canada Ltd, 2801 John Street, Markham, Ontario, Canada L3R 1B4
Penguin Books (N.Z.) Ltd, 182–190 Wairau Road, Auckland 10, New Zealand

First published in the U.S.A. by Macmillan Publishing Co. Inc. 1985 LCCN 86-42772
First published by Faber and Faber 1985
Published in Puffin Books 1987

Printed and bound in Great Britain by
Cox & Wyman Ltd, Reading
Typeset in Sabon

For Leon, Vivien and Jane Garfield,
with love

One

"There is no need for this family to go on holiday," Grandma remarked. "Everything that has happened to us so far in Wales could just as easily have happened at home."

There was some truth in this. So far, the Bagthorpes had hardly set foot out of their rented house, Ty Cilion Duon. It was the third day of their holiday. The police had just left, having taken down sworn (and radically conflicting) statements about the events of the previous night. The two mangled police cars had been towed away, and the one that was merely dented, driven off.

"You realize, don't you," said Mr Bagthorpe, "that that demented goat is still at large?"

Daisy Parker's pet goat, Billy Goat Gruff, liberally festooned with bells and satin bows, had pranced out of a hedge into the path of a police car the previous night. The car had swerved to avoid it and crashed into a tree. (It was not in fact this crash that had rendered the car a write-off, but a second one, minutes later, in the drive of Ty Cilion Duon, where it careered straight into the back of another police car with Daisy at the wheel.)

"I think we all ought to go and look for it," said Rosie, the youngest Bagthorpe. "Poor little Daisy was really upset when she had to go home without him."

This suggestion was met with a total lack of enthusiasm, if not downright hostility.

"With any luck, it'll get run over," said William, the eldest.

"I've more to do than go ferreting round after goats," said Mrs Fosdyke.

"If it *did*," went on William thoughtfully, "could we barbecue it, d'you think?"

Nobody knew whether or not this was a possibility. But given the fact that Ty Cilion Duon's sole cooking facility was a monolithic boiler which had probably not been lit for a century, the Bagthorpes thought the proposition worth considering. Barbecued goat roasted on a spit would certainly make an original dish.

"I 'aven't got 'erbs for goat," said Mrs Fosdyke unhelpfully.

"You can eat their milk and cheese," Jack said. "But I've never actually seen goat on a menu."

"Who'd skin it?" inquired Tess. "Would you, Father?"

Mr Bagthorpe had frequently in the past expressed his urgent wish to skin the goat alive, but now curtly refused to do so dead.

"Any of you who consume the flesh of that beast do so at your own risk," he told his family. "It would be better off buried six foot under, with a stake through its heart."

While the Bagthorpes sat blithely discussing the fate of a goat presumed dead, Billy Goat Gruff, very much alive, was making his entry into the village of Llosilli, less than half a mile away.

Meanwhile, news of the Bagthorpes' recent exploits were being bruited over police radios nationwide, and relayed in countless village pubs over a wide radius.

Any story that is passed around by word of mouth tends to grow in the telling, like a stone collecting barnacles. In Wales, the merest whisper can become like a *moth* collecting barnacles. Even Welsh policemen have a vein of poetry in them, and a taste for judicious decoration. The embroidery that was being done on the latest episode of the Bagthorpe Saga was of a very high order indeed.

Already in some places Daisy Parker was being credited with having written off seven police vehicles. Billy Goat Gruff, who on the night in question had been lavishly decorated with satin ribbons and silver bells, scarcely needed touching up. Most people found him unbelievable as it was. The stories now circulating about him put him right beyond the pale of anything that could possibly be described as natural, and therefore firmly into the misty realms of the supernatural.

"Come dancing out of nowhere from the hedge, he did," Policeman Number Three told the locals in The Welsh Harp. "All white he was, and gleaming, with eyes burning like coals. *Green* coals. And bows on his horns, see, and bells and ribbons—you wouldn't believe!"

"What about his hooves, Ivor?" inquired one listener. "Notice his hooves, did you?"

"Never saw them," Three replied. "Too hypnotized by his eyes, and busy steering."

"And then what did he do, Ivor?"

"Vanished!" This, at least, was true. "Vanished, into thin air!"

This was not true, as people were later to discover to their cost.

Meanwhile, in another pub, Policeman Number Four was giving his version of events. This time, the goat was breathing fire and his eyes were glowing red as traffic lights.

The Bagthorpes, then, were fast becoming Welsh Legend. In the village of Llosilli their name was on all lips. Mr Bagthorpe had already succeeded in arousing hostility down there during preliminary inquiries to track down the Mr Jones who had rented him Ty Cilion Duon. He had glowered murderously at anyone speaking in the Welsh tongue, and made tactless remarks about the name Jones, and about Welsh rugby. These had been intended as light quips, but had raised no smiles. Also, of course, Grandpa had been found dripping wet and lost in the main street at dusk. (This was not as bad as it sounded. The Bagthorpes had only temporarily mislaid him.)

Now, while rumour was fast becoming fact, and fact legend, the Bagthorpes, oblivious of all this, were still holed up in Ty Cilion Duon, taking stock. They were in the kitchen, which still reeked strongly of garlic after the attempted séance of the night before. Mr Bagthorpe, tired of waiting for ghosts to manifest themselves voluntarily, had tried unsuccessfully to summon them.

"Will we have another séance tonight?" asked Jack. He was as keen as anyone for a ghost to appear, so that he could observe Zero's fur standing up on end.

"Oh, please don't let's!" begged Rosie. The revelation that the name Ty Cilion Duon meant House with Black Corners had much alarmed her. According to the elusive Mr Jones the house was haunted by a Veiled Lady, a Small Child Weeping, a Bearded Man Carrying a Candle, a Disembodied Skull, a Ring of Blue Fire emitting a high-pitched wail and an Old Man Limping. This was a lot of ghosts, by any standards. But if every corner in the house was Black, and each with its own spectre, then the tally of ghosts would be truly formidable.

It was Mrs Fosdyke who clinched the matter.

"I'm using that garlic," she informed them, "in a stew. And if you're all going to start tampering with spirits you ought to get a pentagon drawn proper."

"I quite agree, Mrs Fosdyke," put in Grandma. "Henry's typical amateurish approach simply will not do in this instance. It is totally inappropriate. He is quite out of his depth. He is engaging with the dark springs of evil."

"To which you yourself, Mother, are no stranger," he returned.

"We really must try to get back into some kind of regular rhythm today," said Mrs Bagthorpe, with an air of desperate brightness.

Her spouse stared.

"Regular?" he repeated. "Rhythm? *What* regular rhythm, for crying out loud?"

He had a point here. No one who knew the Bagthorpes would ever have described their lives as either regular or rhythmic. Mrs Bagthorpe, however, was an obstinate optimist. This was entirely to her credit. Most people would have had their optimism knocked out of them long before. Mrs Fosdyke (who in any case had embarked on her career with the family with a minimum of this) certainly had.

"I'll *make* the casserole," she now said, "but someone else'll 'ave to watch it. I ain't 'aving any camping stove in my kitchen. They blow up."

"Certainly, Mrs Fosdyke," gushed Mrs Bagthorpe. "I mean – not certainly they blow up – I don't believe they do, or at least, not frequently. But certainly it shall be moved elsewhere, and certainly one of the others will watch it for you."

Her offspring studiously avoided catching her eye. None of them had as yet made any plans as to how to spend the afternoon, but whatever these turned out to be, they certainly would not include watching casseroles. All the Bagthorpes had notoriously low thresholds of boredom, and never watched anything if they could help it.

"And what about the veg?" continued Mrs Fosdyke. "How d'you cook veg on one of them barbicans? Drop 'em raw on to the coals, do you, or what?"

"Oh, it's perfectly simple," Mrs Bagthorpe assured her. "One merely parcels them up in foil, with a little butter and perhaps some herb and seasoning, and they cook beautifully."

"They don't taste of coal, I hope," said Mrs Fosdyke. "And there's no poisonous fumes gets into 'em?"

Mrs Bagthorpe made an abortive attempt at a tinkling laugh. It came out more as a hysterical whinny.

"Never!" she cried. "We have been eating them like that for years, haven't we, everybody?"

The others grudgingly assented, and Mrs Bagthorpe looked anxiously at Mrs Fosdyke, to see whether this testimony was acceptable to her. Mrs Bagthorpe knew that Mrs Fosdyke was understandably disgusted with her present kitchen – indeed, she had gone into severe shock when first confronted by it. It was still on the cards that she would up sticks and go – particularly after the séance of the previous night. If she did, then Mrs Bagthorpe knew from previous experience that she herself would be left to do all the work. Rotas for sharing chores would be drawn up, all right. But all the Bagthorpes – and notably Mr Bagthorpe and Grandma – had a long history of carving rotas to ribbons. Their notions of justice were extremely hazy and ill-defined.

Mrs Bagthorpe's assurance of the harmlessness of barbecued vegetables might have been true, but it was extremely tactless. So far as Mrs Fosdyke was concerned, *she* was cook.

"When?" she demanded suspiciously. "How? How've you been eating 'em for years?"

"Er—we—we have had the occasional barbecue in the evening," faltered Mrs Bagthorpe, realizing her mistake.

"After I've gone home, I s'pose," said Mrs Fosdyke grimly.

Put like that, it did make the Bagthorpes sound sly and mean. They *had* deliberately excluded Mrs Fosdyke from their barbecues, and been careful to eradicate all traces of them. This was partly because they enjoyed messing about with fire and flames and were afraid that Mrs Fosdyke would take charge, and start bossing them about. It was also, quite simply, that by evening they had usually had enough of her.

Fortunately for Mrs Bagthorpe, who was now floundering, the inquiry was halted by the sound of wheels spurting on gravel.

"Uncle Park!" exclaimed Rosie. "Ace! Is Daisy with him?"

She ran out to investigate.

"They've only been gone five minutes," observed Mrs Fosdyke sourly, and with a degree of truth. The Parkers had certainly spent most of the morning at Ty Cilion Duon, making their statements to the police. Mrs Fosdyke had been hoping that Daisy would be locked up. That she had not, seemed to her a clear miscarriage of justice.

The Parkers were staying at a five star hotel, a converted castle, just up the road. Its luxuriousness contrasted starkly with the Bagthorpes' own accommodation, which resembled, as Uncle Parker had himself pointed out, a Victorian doss-house.

"Hullo, all!"

The Bagthorpes turned. They stared.

"Crikey, Uncle Park!" said Jack. "You look as if you've been through a hedge backwards!"

Uncle Parker was a very snappy dresser. He was outstandingly elegant—indeed, Mr Bagthorpe, whose own appearance was usually like that of an ill-made bed, often referred to him as "that gin-swigging tailor's dummy".

On this occasion, Uncle Parker was utterly dishevelled, presumably as a result of combing the undergrowth for the missing Billy Goat Gruff. His outfit had started out being snazzy, you could see that, but its present state would have rendered it unfit even for offer to Oxfam.

"Goat get you, did it?" inquired Mr Bagthorpe, hugely pleased by his old antagonist's disarray.

"Your hand is bleeding!" cried Mrs Bagthorpe. Her husband hastily averted his eyes. He had yesterday been hideously humiliated by fainting in the presence of Mrs Fosdyke at the sight of what he had taken to be blood on his own hand (his writing hand). This had turned out to be red paint, and he knew that he would never hear the last of it. He simply could not afford to faint again in full view of the entire family.

"*I* got blood as well!" squealed Daisy. "*And* my frock got torn and I been crying and crying!"

A single glance at Daisy's tear- and mud-besmirched face and tattered clothing established this to be the truth.

"Look at her poor little legs!" exclaimed Rosie indignantly. "All scratched! Why can't Aunt Celia let her wear jeans, like everyone else?"

"Your Aunt Celia does not see Daisy as a wearer

15

of blue denim, however faded," replied Uncle Parker, predictably rising to the defence of his wife.

"The rest of us," Mr Bagthorpe said, "do not see Daisy as a member of the human race, let alone a wearer of blue denim. And Celia, when she sees the present state of her accursed offspring, will probably finally part company with her marbles. She has been on the verge of doing so for years."

"Yes, well—that's why I've dropped in, don't you know," admitted Uncle Parker. "I thought that if I could get Daisy cleaned up a bit before we go back to the castle, it would soften the blow somewhat. A hot bath, Laura, perhaps. . . ?"

"Oh dear!" exclaimed Mrs Bagthorpe helplessly.

"What she means, Russell," Mr Bagthorpe told him, "is that we do not have such corrupting modern amenities as baths and hot water."

"We've got a *bath*," Jack pointed out.

16

"We have a bath," returned Mr Bagthorpe, "in which one could confidently set out to cross the Atlantic."

"I not going in barf!" screamed Daisy, settling the matter. "I *ate* barfs! And Arry Awk – he 'ates barfs!"

No one much liked the sound of this. Arry Awk, Daisy's invisible friend and accomplice, had of late been conspicuous by his absence, and the Bagthorpes had breathed more freely as a result.

"Look, Daisy, Arry Awk is dead," said Jack. "We had a funeral, remember?"

"He not he not he not!" screamed Daisy.

"He had certainly better be," said Mr Bagthorpe. "I do not imagine that the manager of that five star castle you're stopping in will have taken out insurance to cover your hell-raising daughter, Russell, let alone Arry Awk. I expect that you were congratulating yourself on having lost the goat. It now appears that you have gone straight from the fat to the fire."

He paused.

"And I use the word 'fire'," he added, "advisedly."

A faint frown was, in fact, creasing Uncle Parker's normally unruffled brow.

"We *an't* lost my goat," said Daisy. "We looking for him. An' then there'll be Billy Goat Gruff and Arry Awk and we can play lots and lots of games and look for dragons and ghosties!"

"Hear that, Russell?" said Mr Bagthorpe delightedly. "Quite a catalogue of house guests you'll be entertaining, it seems. I wish you joy of them."

"Darling child," said Grandma to Daisy, "you and I shall have some splendid times together looking for suitable dragons and ghosties. But I do not think we shall require the assistance of Arry Awk."

The truth of the matter was that Grandma was made as nervous as anybody at the prospect of the resurrection of Daisy's invisible friend and accomplice. She was also extremely jealous of his place in Daisy's affections.

"Only *me* can say if Arry Awk's dead," said Daisy obstinately. "And he *not*. I can see him twinkling at me."

"Twinkling, eh?" said Mr Bagthorpe. "*That* sounds ominous, Russell."

"It could be a mirage that you are seeing, Daisy dear," Grandma told her.

The rest looked askance.

"Wales is noted for its mirages," continued Grandma, without turning a hair.

"What's a mirage, Grandma Bag?" asked Daisy, who had been told by her mother always to ask the meaning of words she did not understand.

"It is a—it is an optical illusion," Grandma told her.

"What's an optical illusion, Grandma Bag?"

"It is—it is a kind of figment of the imagination, dear child. And you, of course, have a quite extraordinary imagination."

"What's a fig—?"

"Look!" Mr Bagthorpe interrupted Daisy's relentless questioning. "We do not have all day to squander discussing the metaphysics of Arry Awk. As far as I'm concerned, the matter is perfectly straightforward. He destroys—therefore he exists. He lights fires, smashes crockery, floods houses—you name it—therefore he exists."

"What I mean to say, Daisy," said Grandma,

ignoring him, "is that if you stretch out your hand to *touch* Arry Awk, you will find that he is not there."

"Oooh, like a ghostie!" squealed Daisy, enchanted.

Grandma was momentarily floored. She had not at all intended to say any such thing.

"Darling lickle Arry Awk's a ghostie, Daddy!" burbled the ecstatic child, "and he's goin' to help me and go finding lots and lots *more* ghosties!"

"And Uncle Tom Cobleigh and all . . ." murmured Mr Bagthorpe.

"We've got some ghosties, Daisy," Rosie put in. "You could come and stop here with us and look for them."

This suggestion smartly wiped the smirk off Mr Bagthorpe's face. His wife, seeing Mrs Fosdyke's expression, cried hastily, "Oh no!" Then, not wishing to seem inhospitable, she added lamely, "I really do think that dear Daisy is too young to be exposed to the supernatural."

"Hell," said Mr Bagthorpe, "is her natural habitat. She would strike terror to the heart of any ghost – if there *are* any ghosts in this God-forsaken hole, as that trickster Jones claims, it will be *they* who are frightened, not her. I am engaged in a deadly serious piece of scientific research. I do not –"

"Look," interposed Uncle Parker, "I'm enjoying this conversation no end, but if you could just lead me to some hot water, Laura, and some soap?"

"There's all hot water 'as to be boiled up," said Mrs Fosdyke. "You'll 'ave to wait. That child wants going in a bath, if you ask me."

She did not add "and drowning" but the suggestion seemed implicit in her manner.

"I not I not I not!" Daisy seemed in danger of reverting to her earlier hysteria.

"Does she *never* take a bath, Russell?" inquired Mrs Bagthorpe with a perplexed air.

"Well . . . no . . . not exactly," he admitted. "She—she has this ancient, primitive fear, don't you see?"

"Of what?" demanded Mr Bagthorpe. "Of being clean?"

"Of—of going down the plughole," Uncle Parker admitted shamefacedly.

Hoots and screams of laughter and derision greeted this admission.

"You must be joking!" William said.

"I *not* going down the plughole, I not I not!" screamed Daisy. "And Arry Awk in't, as well! You jus' go round and round and down and down and never come up!"

"And what a mercy *that* would be," commented Mr Bagthorpe. "Come to think, there's a good chance she *would* go down the one upstairs. Go and look it over, Russell, and see what you think."

"It is not, in fact," said Uncle Parker distantly, "a laughing matter. And Celia does not wish it discussed in front of Daisy. It is an ancient, deep-rooted, magical fear, and part of the natural process of development."

"*I* never thought I'd go down the plughole," objected Jack.

"Nor me," added Tess and William simultaneously.

"That is because neither of your parents was teetering on the brink of lunacy," Mr Bagthorpe told them.

"Go down the plughole my foot!" said Tess. "If she believes that, she'll believe anything."

"And does," said Mr Bagthorpe grimly.

"I not listening I not!" Daisy stuck both fingers in her ears and shut her eyes for good measure. "I not even *finking* about it, so there! I finking about darling lickle Billy and dragons and ghosties an'—"

Uncle Parker here cut short this catalogue of his daughter's meditations. He looked as near being unsettled as anyone could remember ever having seen him.

"I'll take Daisy off," he said. "If Celia, who is already under immense nervous strain, becomes unhinged at the sight of her, then I shall know whom to thank. The odd drop of the milk of human kindness would not come amiss in this household."

"The milk of *what*?" repeated William disbelievingly. He honestly did not know what on earth Uncle Parker was talking about.

"I should nip off and get a drop of the hard stuff, Russell," Mr Bagthorpe heartlessly advised him. "*That*'ll take the edge off things. It's like old Eliot says, 'human kind cannot bear very much reality'. In your case, one is bound to admit, reality is exceptionally brutal."

Uncle Parker led away Daisy who, far from having been cleaned up, looked if anything more stained and dishevelled than when she had arrived.

"Funny," said Tess thoughtfully, "how if you go through a hedge backwards in denims it hardly notices. It only notices if you're got up in satin and frills."

That Tess was not using her usual polysyllables was an indication that she had been as thrown by recent events as anyone else, and was not yet herself again.

"That is an interesting observation, darling," said Mrs Bagthorpe, who was desperate for something Positive to say.

"Bilge," said her husband. "You all seem obsessed by the notion that if that evil brat were put into denim she would then automatically become a member of the human race. That is dangerous thinking. It is about as naive as expecting to reform Idi Amin by putting him into a ballet skirt. I do not have time to stand around discussing such half-baked theories. Kindly scatter, all of you. Find something—"

He broke off in mid-flight. Somewhere outside there came the all too familiar sound of a crash. It sounded like two cars colliding.

"It cannot be, of course," Mrs Bagthorpe told herself Positively as they all made for the door. "History simply does not repeat itself in that way."

She was, of course, wrong. There, on the first bend in the drive, were Uncle Parker's red Austin Healey and a police car, blue light flashing. Two officers were already climbing out, shouting and waving their arms about. One of them was stamping his foot.

"Ye gods!" exclaimed Mr Bagthorpe in tones of awe. "She's done it again!"

Two

Policemen are not supposed, of course, to yell and stamp their feet at members of the public. On this occasion, however, any examining magistrates would have been bound to treat the matter with lenience. Numbers Three and Four had been sorely tried during the past sixteen hours and were by now at snapping point. They had already been summoned for an interview with a superior officer later in the day, and were anticipating a thorough carpeting, or worse.

It was fortunate that Uncle Parker, in his haste to escape, had begun to reverse at speed down the drive. (Uncle Parker was a very fast reverser – he reversed faster than some people drive forward.) It was unlucky, however, in that he had not troubled to look in his driving mirror. But had he been driving in a forward gear, although he would certainly have *seen* the approaching police car, he would have been travelling at such a speed that the inevitable crash would have been extremely serious. Even as it was, the resulting damage was no laughing matter (except to Mr Bagthorpe and certain of his unfeeling offspring).

The police had been in no laughing mood even

before the crash. They were speeding towards Ty Cilion Duon to report a sighting of Billy Goat Gruff in Llosilli, and demand that his owners immediately accompany them there to recapture him. Everyone else was too frightened to go near him after hearing the descriptions of him circulated by the police themselves. Some of them thought he might even be the devil incarnate. This view was supported by Mr Bagthorpe.

"Do you have no trained marksmen?" he asked Three and Four when their mission was explained.

"We do not," replied Three bitterly, "and nor, at this rate, shall we soon have any squad cars. The entire force is under threat."

"No one, I hope," put in Grandma, "is going to claim that *this* mishap is the fault of darling Daisy?"

"It is, in a way," Jack said. He had seen Uncle Parker's face when he saw the crumpled state of his beloved car, and felt sorry for him. "It all boils down to Daisy in the end."

"You shut up, Jack Bagthorpe!" Rosie told him. "You're always trying to get her into trouble!"

This was not strictly true. Jack sometimes felt a sneaking admiration and affection for Daisy. Nor, of course, did Daisy require assistance from anybody in the matter of getting into trouble. She did this the whole time, mostly single-handed.

On hearing that her pet had been sighted in the village she chirped up miraculously. (She had also enjoyed the crash, and all the shouting.)

"Quick!" she squeaked. "Quick, Daddy! Me'n Arry Awk want to find Billy!"

As only the rear of Uncle Parker's car had been

damaged the engine was still in working order. The police car, while by no means in showroom condition, also actually started up.

"There is one thing," commented Mr Bagthorpe, as they watched the two vehicles disappear, "Russell is not going to stop in these parts for long, after this little lot. Thank God for that. It is an ill wind . . ."

He returned to the house in a relatively mellow frame of mind. Mr Bagthorpe was not given to mellowness and his offspring, noting his unaccustomed mood, held a whispered conference and decided to produce their still unopened school reports. He took them and retired to the room he had designated as his study. Within two minutes he was out again, waving a fistful of papers.

"I have never in my life read such a load of unadulterated bilge," he said. "I do not believe a single word of it."

The young Bagthorpes held their breath and rolled their eyes at one another. Could it be that their father had finally detected their forgeries?

"He's sussed us!" hissed Rosie to Jack.

"Sssh!" he whispered back. "Just act natural."

"You read 'em, Laura," ordered Mr Bagthorpe, thrusting them at her. Her offspring watched her face anxiously. Her expression was changing rapidly from pride and pleasure to dismay, and back again, as well it might, given that the remarks she was reading had been composed alternately by the teachers and the young Bagthorpes themselves.

"Oh dear!" she said weakly when she had finished. "I don't know what to make of it. But they don't really seem very much different from usual, Henry."

25

(Her children had been adding forged comments to their reports for years.)

"Of course they don't!" he snapped. "That is precisely what I am saying. They are, as usual, bilge. I shall remove the children from those schools."

His offspring let out concerted breaths of relief. Mr Bagthorpe made this threat at the end of every term.

"I must have a desk," he now went on. "I do not see how I can be expected to survive without one. I can rise above most things, Laura, as you know, but no serious creative writer can exist without a desk. I feel as if my very soul has been amputated."

"It was *you* who rented this house, Henry," she told him coldly, "and it is certainly seriously lacking in furnishings."

"'Ow am *I* expected to manage?" Mrs Fosdyke now put her oar in. "'Ere I am, stuck months on end in a kitchen with no draining board, no fridge, no stove, no working surfaces, no Hoover, no dishwasher. . . ."

She went automatically off into the monotonous litany that she had composed while in the state of coma induced by first seeing the kitchen of Ty Cilion Duon.

"I'm properly 'amstrung," she ended.

"Oh dear!" Mrs Bagthorpe was considerably more anxious to conciliate Mrs Fosdyke than she was her husband who had, after all, brought his present troubles on himself. She thought rapidly.

"*I* know!" she exclaimed. "Yes—that's it! It will be the most splendid fun!"

"What will, Laura?" demanded her husband. "Explain yourself!"

"Country sales!" she said. "We shall go to a country auction and purchase any furniture and utensils we require!"

"Which will finally bankrupt me," Mr Bagthorpe said.

"Wales must be full of decaying country houses," went on his wife.

"We're *in* one," he reminded her.

"And I expect that their contents are auctioned at

27

extremely reasonable prices," she continued, evidently fired by her inspiration. "Someone must go straight to the village and buy a local newspaper."

"*I* will!" volunteered all her children as one. With any luck, Billy Goat Gruff would still be on the rampage in the village and there would be plenty of action.

"Very well," said Mrs Bagthorpe, to their surprise. "You may all go. You have had very little exercise since we arrived, and the fresh air will do you good.".

"When you come back, bring the telephone directory back with you," Mr Bagthorpe told them.

"What – you mean take it out of the kiosk?" Jack was shocked.

"Where else?" he returned. "Do I have to spell out everything twice?"

"You cannot possibly ask the children to do any such thing," Mrs Bagthorpe told him crossly. "The telephone directory is the property of British Telecom. You are inciting them to a felony."

"You are not on the Bench now, Laura," he returned. "We are not *stealing* the directory. We are merely borrowing it."

"For how long?" asked Rosie.

"For as long as it takes to count the number of Joneses in it," he replied.

Everyone gaped.

"But there must be dozens!" said Rosie. "Hundreds!"

"You, Rosie, are always making extravagant claims about your mathematical genius," he told her. "You now have an opportunity to display it."

"How?" she demanded.

"You will calculate (a) the number of Joneses in the directory and (b) the exact cost of telephoning them all. Calculate it on the basis of two minutes per call. Then (c) calculate how long it will take."

"But it'd be hours," said Tess.

"Days," said William.

"Weeks," added Jack.

"I am not interested in your wild guesses," he told them. "I want exact figures. I shall need a bill to present to that trickster Jones when I finally track him down."

"Well, *I'm* not pinching the 'phone book out of the kiosk," Rosie told him. "*I* don't want to end up in prison, thanks."

"Nor me," said her siblings in unison. They were not for a moment considering the inconvenience that would be caused to the general public by such an action. They were, as usual, thinking of their own skins.

"Then you can camp out in the kiosk till you've done the sums," Mr Bagthorpe said. "Take some sandwiches."

"And a camp bed, I suppose," said William.

A moderate furore then set up in which everyone, with the exception of Mrs Fosdyke, took part. She expressed her own feelings by banging about in the contents of her Portable Pantry, and snorting. In the end it was decided that Rosie would spend as long in the kiosk as it took to count the total number of columns of Joneses in the directory. She would then count the number of lines per column. Armed with this information she could then return to Ty Cilion Duon and do the more complicated sums on her calculator.

"I don't care how you do it," Mr Bagthorpe told her. "Just do it."

"Come on," said Jack impatiently, "let's go!"

He was afraid that the fun with the goat would be all over if they didn't move quickly.

"You'd best fetch back a load of garlic," Mrs Fosdyke said. She felt that garlic was likely to be her most potent ally in the confrontation with the supernatural that Mr Bagthorpe was planning.

"And some chalk," she added. "I'm 'aving a pentagon, I am."

The four of them set off at a run for Llosilli in gleeful anticipation of the chase.

They were not disappointed.

Billy Goat Gruff had emerged from the undergrowth around midday. He had had a quiet night (which was more than anyone else had had) and breakfasted happily on the nearby herbage. At length, however, he had become restless. It might have been his living in such close proximity to the Bagthorpes, or it might just be that all goats have low thresholds of boredom, but whatever the reason he had set off in search of action. If there *was* none, then he would create some.

His appearance alone was sufficient to galvanize the inhabitants of Llosilli. Their hitherto quiet lives had already been considerably shaken up since the advent of the Bagthorpes. Even those who had not yet personally encountered them felt threatened and edgy.

When Billy Goat Gruff pranced into the High Street, jingling bells and a-flutter with bows and satin streamers, panic swept through the village. The streets emptied, doors banged shut, the Post Office switchboard was jammed with calls made by people ringing to warn relatives or friends. It was some time before anyone managed to get through to the police.

Windows (mainly upper ones) were thrown open as the goat made his jaunty way down the middle of the road.

"It was just like looking out and seeing Santa Claus go by," said one resident later. "Or the Loch Ness Monster."

An unfortunate motorist who happened to be passing through evidently thought the same. He rounded a bend, saw the goat, swerved violently and hit a lamppost. He sat there, dazed and trembling. Then he saw Billy Goat Gruff's bearded and beribboned face and curious yellow eyes within inches of his window. He moaned, closed his eyes and went into a faint. This, then, was the goat's first victim. The siege of Llosilli had begun.

Three

It was unfortunate that Billy Goat Gruff's first visit
was to the Police House itself. He could not possibly
have known this, but Mr Bagthorpe always maintained afterwards that he had.

"A primordial satanic instinct led him there," he
would say. "He sniffed it out, like a werewolf making
straight for the jugular. He twice went for mine, if you
remember."

The goat did not in fact do anything quite so drastic
as this. He did, however, create a fair measure of
havoc. He tripped through the open gate and down
the side of the house. The back door was standing
ajar. Accordingly he trotted inside, where Mrs Henwick was preparing to feed the baby.

It is difficult to say who was the more surprised. It
was a toss-up. For a few seconds the pair stared at one
another. As a policeman's wife, Mrs Henwick was
accustomed to having some queer customers in her
kitchen from time to time, but had not so far
encountered a goat. Nor, of course, was Billy Goat
Gruff in any way run-of-the-mill in appearance. Most
goats in Wales go around as Nature intended them.
Billy Goat Gruff, with his silver bells and satin bows

and drapes, went around as Daisy Parker intended him.

Mrs Henwick had heard all about the Bagthorpes and the Parkers from her husband, so at least she knew instantly what this apparition was. She had no wish for either herself or her baby to be killed, or even chewed. Accordingly she took evasive action. She moved fast. Clutching the baby, she ran into the hall and slammed the door behind her. There she stood breathing heavily and listening.

At first there was silence. Then various noises could be heard. At first there was only the odd clatter and clink that meant that the goat was investigating her kitchen. Then came an almighty crash. This, Mrs Henwick suspected, meant that her Welsh hot-pot, intended for supper, had hit the tiles. The thought of the goat in there happily scoffing it maddened her. She put the baby down on the rug and cast about for a suitable weapon.

"I'll fetch him one with the warming pan," she decided.

She took it from the wall and ran back into the kitchen brandishing it. The goat did not, as she had expected, turn tail. She was not to know that he was used to conducting fights rather on the lines of a Spanish bullfight. As a rule, he won. It was others who turned tail.

This occasion was to be no exception. Mrs Henwick spent the next few minutes running in circles round the kitchen table taking fruitless swipes with the copper warming pan. These were fruitless only in the sense that they did not land on Billy Goat Gruff. By the end of the bout the Welsh dresser was quite bare and the floor ankle-deep in smashed blue and white crockery.

In the end Billy Goat Gruff became bored and dizzy, and ran out through the back door. In the garden he careered into a line of washing which became entwined in his horns. When he next appeared in the street he was swathed in a white sheet in addition to his existing trinkets. His progress was severely impeded by this, forcing him to execute wild, lunging movements. To the horrified eyes in the windows this created an even stronger impression of dementia.

"Has 'e killed Mrs Henwick?"

"The baby—eaten it, has he?"

These and similar speculations were called from window to window. By the time they reached the lower end of the High Street both Mrs Henwick and her baby had become mangled corpses.

At the top end, however, these rumours were shortly given the lie by the appearance of the enraged Mrs Henwick, still brandishing her warming pan and in hot pursuit of the goat and her sheet. This gave the entirely erroneous impression that she had routed the goat and that he was running away from her. Thus encouraged, certain of the bolder spirits of Llosilli armed themselves with pokers, garden rakes and brooms, and joined the pursuit.

What followed was rather on the lines of the sort of fairy tale where a gingerbread man, or a goose, or such, collects a whole string of pursuers. There were differences, however. By the time the goat was half way down the High Street he had collected around two dozen pursuers, whereas most fairy tales stick at less than half that number. And fairy tales, of course, usually have happy endings.

Probably none of the valiant villagers wielding their brooms and brollies had any clear idea of what they would do if they actually caught their quarry. They had joined in under the influence of a kind of mass hysteria, and possibly with a vague feeling that there was safety in numbers. Pell mell they went, legs going like clockwork, and uttering warlike cries.

When the goat stopped dead in his tracks there was a very nasty pile-up. The front runners skidded to an abrupt halt and those behind ploughed into them at speed. Within seconds the strung-out procession had reduced itself to an untidy heap of bodies with arms, legs, rakes and pokers sticking out at angles. It looked like the kind of composition that receives large subsidies from the Arts Council.

The horrified inmates of Llosilli hanging out of their windows waited, breath held. Many of them had friends and loved ones in that heap. The goat, after only fractional hesitation, charged. Afterwards everyone in the pile-up claimed to have received a direct butt. Given that the goat charged only three times this

35

was clearly impossible. The cuts and bruises sustained were mainly inflicted by their own assorted weaponry.

At amazing speed the heap resolved itself again into individuals who, to a man, turned tail and scampered off up the High Street twice as fast as they had come down. They scattered and ran to the nearest houses, battering on the doors and yelling to be let in. The unfortunate Mrs Henwick who, as front runner, had ended up at the bottom of the pile, was last up, and singled out by the goat as his prime target.

It was at this stage that the police and Uncle Parker arrived. This was lucky for Mrs Henwick because she was by now seriously out of puff and would almost inevitably have been martyred. She ran to the police car, wrenched open the door and fell inside. Simultaneously Daisy leapt from her seat and ran towards her pet.

"Oh my darling lickle Billy!" she squealed. "What those naughty people wrapped you in?"

She was referring to the sheet, which by now would patently have to be torn up for cleaning rags, the goat himself having already begun this exercise. She tugged at the trailing tatters, watched by an audience confident that they were now about to witness a killing.

To their astonishment, however, the goat was behaving rather in the manner of the transmogrified Bottom with Titania. He was nuzzling Daisy and giving her little playful nudges and skipping on the spot.

It was unfortunate, therefore, that at this juncture an ambulance, with a fire engine in hot pursuit, came screaming down the High Street with every available siren and flashing light brought into play. Billy Goat

Gruff's life with the Parkers could not have been described as quiet, but even he was not used to a racket of this order. (He had missed Daisy's fire-raising Phase.)

He rolled his eyes, emitted a high-pitched juddering bleat, and bolted. Daisy, still clutching a fragment of the sheet, was jerked violently and pitched forward on to her face.

The confusion that followed was extreme and no coherent picture of it ever emerged. It was still reigning when the Bagthorpe contingent came tearing into the top of the village, having been overtaken by the emergency services and redoubled their pace. If there was to be fire, flood and the shedding of blood, they wanted to see it.

By then, at the exhortation of various villagers, the firemen had connected their hoses, despite the total absence of fire.

"Use 'em like a cannon!" they were advised. "It's a riot!"

"Testing!" yelled the chief fireman, and two jets of water shot into the air and then descended as a heavy drizzle on the firemen themselves and the Parkers, who were the only ones left, everybody else having run for cover.

Daisy, scrambling to her feet, was enchanted by this new development, which reminded her of home.

"Let *me* shoot the water," she pleaded, "and Arry Awk—let *him* shoot one!"

She had made similar requests before, when the local brigade had come to put out her fires, but these had always been curtly refused. Daisy, however, was a born trier. She tugged so hard on one fireman's arm

37

that he lost his aim and directed his jet full on to the advancing Bagthorpes. They shrieked and scattered but were instantly drenched to the skin. William, enraged, ran forward and began tugging at Daisy, who was still tugging at the fireman. She turned and, without losing her hold, delivered a series of sharp kicks to his shin that forced him to retreat.

"Look out! Look out!" yelled voices from nearby windows. "There's a mad goat loose! Take cover!"

The Bagthorpes had a healthy respect for Billy Goat Gruff's powers of destruction but did not seriously consider him a threat to life, and ignored this advice.

"Where *is* the goat?" demanded Tess.

Nobody knew. All present had been too busy saving their own skins to notice which way the goat had gone. Heads swivelled. The firemen wheeled warily about, their hoses playing. They stood thus aimlessly spraying for some time, until they began to feel silly. Firemen are used to urgent action, not standing around being human fountains. Having Daisy Parker skipping about among them squeaking and tugging at their arms made the situation even more farcical. The Bagthorpes had retreated out of range of the spray and were hopping about uncomfortably in their soaked clothes.

"W-where is the g-goat, d'you think?" Jack asked. His teeth were chattering already. No one knew, though they all kept busy looking. He could come charging at them from any direction at any moment.

The police car had now turned and was racing back up the High Street to retrieve Mrs Henwick's abandoned baby and investigate the car wrapped round the lamppost. Seeing this, the firemen decided that the emergency had passed, and turned off their hoses.

A queer, nervous hush then descended. The Parkers and the Bagthorpes, as the only persons now on the scene in any active sense, felt rather like actors stranded on a stage without a script. They were conscious of the eyes watching from every window. Jack found himself half hoping that Billy Goat Gruff would reappear and provide some action for them. All there was to see at present was Daisy Parker running round and round the fire engine squealing:

"Silly men, silly men, switch the water on again!" over and over again, like the refrain of some old ballad.

"Look, Daisy," said Uncle Parker, "let's go back home, shall we? Billy Goat Gruff'll find his way back when he's ready."

He did not for one moment believe this, and certainly did not desire it. He was worried that his wife, left so long alone, might be going into a downward spiral, and become unhinged. It was hard enough to keep her on an even keel at the best of times.

To everybody's surprise, Daisy consented.

"Awwight, Daddy," she agreed. "Billy Goat Gruff's going to find his way home, bringing his tail behind him. And I's hungry."

Uncle Parker thankfully retreated to the shelter of his (admittedly now battered) sports car, bearing Daisy with him. He was afraid that the natives might get ugly. The watching pairs of eyes were all cold as pebbles, and he had a vague notion that the Welsh were fighters. Uncle Parker was not a fighting man. It was not, he would airily tell people, his style, and quite often meant that one's clothes would be

disarranged, or even spoilt. He affected to despise Mr
Bagthorpe, who had been known to have the odd
skirmish.

"You have no natural authority, Henry," he told
him. "Winston Churchill would not have condescen-
ded to brawl, nor Bertrand Russell."

"We'd better go and get those local papers for
Mother," William said as they watched Uncle Parker
make his exit. (His style was considerably cramped by
the crumpled condition of his boot and the presence
of the police higher up the street. Normally when he
knew he had an audience, he would rev through from
standing to eighty miles an hour in four seconds flat.)

The Bagthorpes' reception in the newsagents was
frosty. They stood making puddles on the floor. The
owner peered cautiously round the door from the rear
of the shop, where he had retreated when the goat
appeared.

"You the English, are you, stopping at Ty Cilion
Duon?" he asked.

They replied that they were.

His suspicions confirmed, he said, "You'll not be stopping long?"

He did not add "I hope", but they knew that was what he meant, all right.

"Just till we see some ghosts," Rosie told him.

"It's hell up there," William added. "Father's furious. He's going to take Jones to court when he tracks him down."

The newsagent made a mental note to ring his friend and warn him of this. Mr Jones had already had several such calls.

"That reminds me – the 'phone book!" Rosie said, and shot off.

As the other three drew level with the Post Office, William said, "We shan't be able to pinch the 'phone book anyway, now."

He was referring to the fact that the police were on the other side of the road interviewing the motorist whose car was wrapped round the lamppost. The Bagthorpes could catch snatches of what was being said, and realized that fresh descriptions of Billy Goat Gruff would soon be in circulation.

Rosie came out of the 'phone box.

"What's up, Rosie?" asked Jack anxiously. The others stared. Her face was perfectly white, her eyes were wide and popping. When she first opened her mouth, nothing came out.

"I can't believe it!" she said at length.

"What?" Jack demanded.

"Forty-nine pages. That's ninety-eight sides. Three columns to every side. A hundred and twenty-five Joneses in every column."

There was a brief pause.

"I make that thirty-six thousand seven hundred and fifty," said William.

"Me too," said Rosie bleakly.

"Crikey!" Jack exclaimed, "You mean that's how many Joneses Father has to ring to track *our* Jones down?"

"It would be, if he was the last one in the book," said William. "If his Christian name happens to be Zachariah—which it easily could be, him being Welsh. Good old Baptist name that, I expect."

"Or William," put in Tess. "That'd be pretty expensive."

They all stood and pondered the situation.

"Father'll go spare," William said.

This was unarguable. They could even sympathize with him. Nobody had till now realized how thoroughly Wales is populated with Joneses.

They set off at a leisurely pace for Ty Cilion Duon, despite their wet things. Nobody was in any hurry to get back and break the news to Mr Bagthorpe. They were unusually silent. Each was engaged in a dizzying calculation (or, in Jack's case, speculation) as to the expense involved if Mr Jones's name *did* happen to be Zachariah.

"Or Zebedee," said Rosie as they turned into the drive.

She said it right out of the blue, but everybody knew what she meant.

"Hang on a minute," William said. "How much *is* a local call? I've been calculating at two pence."

"You're miles out, then," Rosie told him. "It's five. Don't you remember? Father rang up the operator to find out after you'd been on to Philip Robinson for about five hours, trying to hypnotize him over the 'phone, Tess."

They *did* remember – and Tess in particular. She had had her pocket-money docked for two weeks.

"And if you go even one second over two minutes," Rosie continued, "it's ten pence, I think."

"We'll calculate it at that," William said. "It'll be easier. Just add a nought on. That's three hundred and sixty seven thousand five hundred."

"Pence," put in Rosie.

"Pence," he agreed. "Which is three thousand six hundred and seventy-five – pounds."

An awed silence followed. The Bagthorpes were not easily awestruck, but they were now.

"Bags not tell Father," said Rosie at length.

"It was you he asked," William said. "You'll have to. And I've thought of something else."

They looked at him inquiringly.

"You'd better calculate how many hours he's going to have to spend in that 'phone box," he said.

"Hours?" echoed Tess. "Weeks, more like. Months."

"And that's if he gets through to them all first time," added Jack. This was a wise thought, and he was pleased with it.

"You'd better calculate first how long it takes to dial the number," William continued, "then allow for the 'phone to ring – say an average of fifteen times, then around two minutes for the actual conversation."

"I think Father might actually be driven insane," said Rosie.

"And there'll be some jolly long queues outside the

43

'phone box," said Jack. He felt that he was making some very pertinent points which more than compensated for his weakness on the calculation side.

"Look," said William, "I'll tell you what, Rosie. We'll all go barging in and create a diversion, and you shoot off upstairs and work it all out on your calculator. And with any luck something'll have happened while we were out to take Father's mind off it."

"What—the camping stove blown up?" said Jack.

"That is not funny," William told him. "Nothing to do with food is funny. I'm going to have a go at cleaning up that old cooking range. You realize, don't you, that if Fozzy hasn't got an oven we'll have to go weeks and weeks without cakes and roasts and stuff?"

They all nodded, taking in this sombre truth.

"Father won't budge from here until he's tracked down Jones," William said. "You know what he's like."

They did. Mr Bagthorpe was magnificently obstinate. He got it from Grandma. He pursued his projects with an obsessive single-mindedness that was possibly his only trait in common with a saint. Once he was bent on anything, to try to stop him was as hopeless as attempting to halt an avalanche in its tracks. More hopeless, if anything. His offspring heaved concerted heavy sighs, and trudged onwards to the house.

Four

Ty Cilion Duon was uncannily quiet. It was easy enough to imagine a few dozen ghosts in there, lurking in all the Black Corners. It was less easy to imagine Mr Bagthorpe, for instance, or Mrs Fosdyke, or Grandma. All three were formidable producers of noise. Mrs Fosdyke was at present severely handicapped in this department by the lack of a Hoover, or even a draining board, but she was already beginning to devise new means of setting up a good rattle. She rummaged about in her Portable Pantry for all the world like a terrier going after a rat. She was also finding that a broom, strategically deployed, could be as effective as any Hoover in disrupting Mr Bagthorpe when he was trying to Create.

"Come on, everyone," William told the others. "We'll make a diversion—you shoot upstairs, Rosie."

Jack's eye fell on the water butt. It was still nearly full, despite Mrs Fosdyke's having squeezed several gallons of water from it over Mrs Bagthorpe the previous night, when she fainted in the drive.

"Let's wet ourselves a bit," he suggested. "Make ourselves really dripping again. That'll take their mind off things."

"Good idea," said Rosie. She went and began splashing herself, and Jack followed suit.

"Two of us dripping'll be enough," William said. "Got a horrible greenish look, that water has, and probably full of beetles and pollywogs."

At this Rosie let out a genuine scream. All four of them charged in through the front door yelling such things as, "Strewth, I'm soaked!", "Daisy's got the fire brigade out again!" and "It's a National Emergency!"

It was unfortunate for them that Mr Bagthorpe had retired to his makeshift study only minutes earlier with instructions that there was to be absolute silence until further notice. This was because he was going to Draw Himself Up, he said.

"What exactly is that, dear?" inquired his wife a little nervously. It sounded rather like hanging.

"I mean, Laura," he told her, "that I am going to Draw Upon my powerful mental and psychic reserves in order to prepare myself for tonight's Calling Up of the Spirits."

"You *have* no mental and psychic reserves, Henry," Grandma told him. "Any that you might once have had you have long ago dissipated. Though I could, of course, teach you to Breathe, I suppose."

"I have no wish to breathe!" he snapped. "Just keep quiet, the lot of you!"

He stamped into his study and slammed the door. Mrs Fosdyke and Grandma both instantly began thinking of ways in which they could drum up a noise. They were forestalled by the entry of the younger Bagthorpes, who clattered across the hall and burst into the kitchen.

"Heavens, darlings, what has happened?" cried Mrs Bagthorpe.

"Is it raining?" inquired Grandma.

"Rain ain't green," Mrs Fosdyke observed sourly. "Not even in Wales. Look at all that green on 'em. And all over my floor!"

Even in her present state of agitation Mrs Bagthorpe could not help noticing Mrs Fosdyke's use of the possessive. If she was beginning to think of the floors of Ty Cilion Duon as *hers*, it could be an encouraging Sign. Mrs Bagthorpe tended to Think Positively even in an emergency.

"We've been soaked by the Fire Brigade," said William. "Daisy's got the Fire Brigade out now, as well as the police."

"Billy Goat Gruff's loose again," said Jack. "He's gone berserk, and everyone's locked up in their houses."

"In *his* house," corrected Mrs Bagthorpe automatically. "Oh dear – and look at the state of you!"

"First time *I've* ever heard of a Fire Brigade with green water," commented Mrs Fosdyke suspiciously. It had evidently been too dark the previous night for her to discern the livid emerald of the water with which she had soused her employer.

At this point Mr Bagthorpe entered, having presumably abandoned his Drawing Up.

"What in the name of – ?" He broke off. He stared speechless for several seconds at his children, who resembled the offspring of Neptune, if anyone's.

When he did speak again his voice was very carefully controlled – always a bad sign.

"Correct me if I am wrong," he said, "but I was

47

under the impression that you had gone to the village to obtain certain information about telephone numbers."

"And to obtain the local papers," put in Mrs Bagthorpe.

"Me 'n Mrs Bagthorpe's after a draining board," supplied Mrs Fosdyke.

"Neither of these missions," continued Mr Bagthorpe, "required you to dive head first into a mountain bog."

They all set up a further clamour, giving him the latest information on the goat front, and thus hoping to delay the evil moment when he would discover that ringing Joneses was the hobby of millionaires.

"Look," he interrupted. "I am not interested in that brat and her exploits. Give me the figures."

"Rosie's just nipped upstairs to work the details out," William stalled.

"Right!" Mr Bagthorpe flung out. His footsteps echoed in the stone hall and up the bare boards of the stairs.

Jack, thinking of poor Rosie up there about to break the news alone, quailed. He also felt rather mean.

"Is there any dinner?" asked William hopefully.

"It's cheese and salad," Mrs Fosdyke told him.

"I thought it was stew," Jack said.

"You wasn't here to light *that*." She jerked her head towards the camping stove. "I don't know how long I shall be able to stand this."

They exchanged glances.

"Stuck here in Wales for weeks on end, hiding my bush under a shovel," continued Mrs Fosdyke, swishing about in her cracked sink.

48

There came from above the anticipated yell of rage.

"It is a pity," remarked Grandma, "that Henry cries 'Wolf!' so often."

"This time," Jack told her, "I think it really *is* wolf!"

When Mr Bagthorpe returned he looked on the verge of apoplexy.

"Four thousand pounds! As near as dammit four thousand! It'll bankrupt me!"

"I've just thought of something," Jack said. "The coin box won't hold all that. It'll have to be emptied about ten times a day."

"We shall have to throw ourselves on the State," Mr Bagthorpe continued.

"What is the matter, Henry dear?" asked Mrs Bagthorpe.

By now he was gibbering. Even had he been able to give a rational explanation for his agitation it would have been all but inaudible. Mrs Fosdyke was rattling pots in the sink as only she knew how. It was her way of joining in the conversation. The more Mr Bagthorpe clamoured for attention, the louder she rattled. He glowered at her back which was, he maintained, the only back he knew able to express pure malevolence.

"That woman leaves Medusa standing," he would declare. "If ever I am found turned to stone, you will know where to look. The only difference is, I pay her wages. There is no record of anyone ever paying *Medusa* wages."

Rosie had now appeared and passed over her calculations to her mother. Mrs Bagthorpe's brow creased. For a long time she did not say anything. On

49

this occasion even she was hard put to it to find anything Positive to say.

"Oh dear!" she said weakly at last. "It does seem rather a lot!"

Mr Bagthorpe was by now listening to nobody. He was rambling on about inbreeding and madness, and about his rates and taxes.

"That's it!" He gave a triumphant cry. "That's it! The police! What am I paying taxes for? It's a criminal investigation! The police'll have to track him down."

He looked about him for some sign of assent from his family. He was met by expressions that were sad, if not downright hopeless. He seemed to have forgotten that the entire Welsh police force had by now heard about the Bagthorpes and many of them had been actively, and disastrously, involved.

"The Welsh police force is 'opeless," remarked Mrs Fosdyke in the ensuing silence. "Else they'd have locked up that Daisy Parker while they 'ad chance."

After this last remark it seemed on the cards that the Welsh police would have a murder to investigate, judging by Mr Bagthorpe's expression.

A wrangle then set up between Mr Bagthorpe and Grandma about the ins and outs of setting the police on to the elusive Mr Jones. The younger Bagthorpes exchanged looks and let out sighs of relief. The crisis had passed. Their father had abandoned all idea of embarking on a telephone marathon that would at least have earned him a place in the *Guinness Book of Records*, if not eventual contact with Mr Jones.

"I shall go straight down to Llosilli and lodge my complaint," he said. "The rest of you can get ready for tonight."

"You'd best all have your dinners first," said Mrs Fosdyke. "Else the washing up'll drag on all afternoon. I should never've believed it if anyone'd told me I should end up without a dishwasher. No dishwasher, no draining board, no working surfaces. . . ."

"*We* will do the washing up," Mrs Bagthorpe interrupted.

At all costs Mrs Fosdyke must be prevented from starting to chant her monotonous litany of missing kitchen equipment. It could act like a mantra, and send her off into an irreversible trance. It had already sent her into a reversible one.

After a light and cheerless lunch Mr Bagthorpe set off for the village, and the rest of the family, the washing up done, scattered to follow their various pursuits.

"I should like another hypnotic session, Tess dear," said Grandma. The thought of ghosts coming out at her from every Black Corner was making her nervous.

"I've got a lot of other important things to do," Tess told her. "I'll teach you *self*-hypnosis, and then you can do it yourself."

The pair disappeared.

"I'm going to tune up my recording equipment," William said. "Sometimes, spirit voices come out on blank tapes, even if nobody's heard a thing."

"Oooh! Do they? Really?" Rosie's voice came out as a squeak. Even Jack, who was looking forward to seeing his dog Zero's fur stand up on end, did not much like the sound of this.

"Oh Mother," cried Rosie," can I go down to the shop and get some more light bulbs?"

"There's only light'll drive out the powers of the dark," remarked Mrs Fosdyke profoundly. "I'll come with you, Rosie. I ain't even *seen* this village yet. Supposed to be a holiday, I thought."

"Ah!" cried Mrs Bagthorpe, rattling her newspaper. "Eureka!"

The others looked at her inquiringly.

"Oh, there are some perfectly *splendid* sales!" she exclaimed. "I can see that at a glance. What fun we shall have! Oh—look at *this* one—Welsh dressers, porcelain, oils, watercolours—"

"What about draining boards?" demanded Mrs Fosdyke. "Does it mention draining boards?"

"Ah, well . . . not in so many *words*, Mrs Fosdyke," admitted Mrs Bagthorpe. "But . . . oh yes . . . 'All Household Effects . . . dishwashers, refrigerators, Hoovers—'"

"Ooo—'Oovers!" Mrs Fosdyke brightened instantly.

"There—we have no carpets," her employer reminded her.

"Hmph!" Mrs Fosdyke snorted disgustedly. "No more we 'ain't. Well, then – carpets. Does it mention carpets?"

"Well . . ." Mrs Bagthorpe was glad that her husband was not present to overhear this conversation. Mrs Fosdyke now seemed hellbent on refurbishing the entire house. There *were* carpets mentioned in the sale notice, but they were Persian, Aubusson and washed Chinese, mostly.

"Let's see . . . when. . . ? Oh, it's tomorrow!" she exclaimed, avoiding the issue.

"That's something, then," conceded Mrs Fosdyke grudgingly. "There's a limit to 'ow long folk go on without draining boards."

Jack wished she would shut up about draining boards. She was getting on his nerves. Though when she *did* acquire one, he reflected, she would get on his nerves even more, and on everyone else's, for that matter. He hoped that it would not be of the reverberating stainless steel variety. Mrs Fosdyke was a virtuoso on the draining board.

Mrs Bagthorpe went off to write letters. She had not intended to work on her Problems while on holiday, but was now sending off a request for them to be forwarded to her. She could then lose herself in them, she thought.

Jack decided that he would take Zero on a tour of Ty Cilion Duon, and get him to have a good sniff in every single Black Corner. If dogs could sniff gelignite undetectable by the human nose, there was a good chance that they could sniff ghosts, too. He was undeterred by its being broad daylight.

"Ghosts must go *somewhere* in the afternoons," he argued.

Rosie and Mrs Fosdyke set off for Llosilli. Both of them were glad to be out of the house, and got along quite happily and companionably. Mrs Fosdyke had a soft spot for Rosie, as the baby of the family. She had had a soft spot for all the Bagthorpe children when they *were* babies. She doted on anything in a pram. It was when they grew older that she went off them.

Rosie, holding the shopping bags, skipped along at Mrs Fosdyke's side.

"It's very pretty round here, isn't it?" she said. "It *seems* like proper Abroad, with all the mountains."

"You want to take good big sniffs while you're 'ere." Mrs Fosdyke advised her. "It's good for your lungs, mountain air."

She demonstrated this by taking an almighty snuff of it herself. Rosie was somewhat alarmed by this. It was bad enough having Grandma pontificating non-stop about Breathing. Nonetheless she obligingly took a few noisy sniffs herself before attempting a change of subject.

At this point they met Mr Bagthorpe. He was bashing up the road at an unprecedented rate, muttering under his breath, after an extremely unsatisfactory interview with the police.

"Father!" called Rosie gaily. He would otherwise have passed them. He looked up and glowered.

"We're going to get some more light bulbs," Rosie told him, but he had already passed them. He had no time for the small courtesies of civilized life. His manners were appalling. The only thing to be said in his defence was that had Rosie and Mrs Fosdyke been belted earls they would have been accorded the same treatment.

When they entered the village shop it was extremely crowded and noisy. A meeting was being held. The babble died away as the presence of two strangers was noticed, but not before Rosie had caught such words as 'goat', 'mad', 'black magic' and 'English'. Mrs Fosdyke had evidently caught them, too. She charged in without preliminary.

"Got that goat yet, 'ave they?" she inquired.

Twenty or so suspicious Welsh gazes fastened on her.

"Er – and why is it you ask?" said the shopkeeper, who was evidently unofficial chairman of the meeting.

"That goat," replied Mrs Fosdyke, "is the most evil, cross-grained creature that ever went on four legs. What it wants is shooting, right between its two horns!"

This forthright statement had her audience quite perplexed. They had correctly put her down as being one of the present occupiers of Ty Cilion Duon and thus, automatically, one of the Enemy. It now appeared that her sentiments, at least on the subject of the goat, matched their own.

"If I 'ad a gun," continued Mrs Fosdyke, sensing that she had an audience, and enjoying it, "and wasn't allergic to loud noises, I'd do it myself!"

"Right you are!" came several heartfelt rejoinders, and "Wouldn't I just, indeed!"

"Well," said the bemused shopkeeper, "that is certainly what we have just now been saying among ourselves, Mrs – er – Bagthorpe?"

The shopkeeper had already, of course, met the real Mrs Bagthorpe, and taken a cheque from her, the previous day. There was no reason, however, why this stranger should not be yet another. No one as yet knew the full extent of the visiting clan. The police, when asked, had fervently given their view that there were at least twenty of them up there. The Bagthorpes, because they moved around so fast and made so much noise, often gave the illusion of being twice as many as they actually were.

Mrs Fosdyke hastened to correct this error.

"Bagthorpe?" she echoed. "*Me*? I should hope not! Gladys Glenys Fosdyke, if you please, and no relation at all, thank you very much! Bagthorpe indeed!"

Rosie was shocked by this treachery. The meeting, on the other hand, was much encouraged by this heartfelt denial, and also by hearing so unimpeachably Welsh a name as Glenys. (Mrs Fosdyke had not a drop of Welsh blood in her veins. She had been named after the heroine of a magazine serial her mother had been reading at the time of her birth.)

In no time at all Mrs Fosdyke was taken to the bosom of the eager throng, and was giving information and opinions left and right. None of this was flattering to the Bagthorpes. The disgusted Rosie marched to the shelves, collected a dozen light bulbs, paid for them and left. She did not bother to tell Mrs Fosdyke that she was leaving.

"If they'd known *I* was a Bagthorpe, I could've been lynched!" she thought indignantly.

A sudden thought struck her.

"They never thought she was my mother!"

She was half tempted to return to the shop to deny all relationship with Mrs Fosdyke.

"But if I did," she thought, "I'd probably have to walk back with her. Rotten sneaky thing. I bet she's telling them all kinds of whoppers about poor little Daisy. I'm never going to speak to her again. I'll eat her food, but I'm not speaking to her!"

She trudged homeward, bitterly reflecting that the holiday they were having bore no resemblance whatever to the advertisements she had seen in magazines and on television.

"You never even *see* ghosts mentioned," she thought. "And we've got them in every corner."

She gave further thought to this, and then came up with something that gave her some comfort.

"When *our* family's dead," she reflected, "I bet *we* all come back as ghosts. Especially Father. I bet Unicorn House has to be exorcized."

Even this, however, was little consolation to poor Rosie, who dreaded the thought that night must eventually fall, and the Black Corners of Ty Cilion Duon let loose their ghostly secrets.

Five

Supper was an altogether more cheerful meal than lunch had been. For one thing, Mrs Fosdyke had made a stew. This was so delicious that no one really worried about its having been cooked in an old outside privy (and its creator, fortunately, did not know this). Jack had set up his camping stove in there because of the wind. Mrs Fosdyke still would not have it in the house. No one even noticed the absence of garlic which Mrs Fosdyke, despite her previous announcement, had decided to save as protection against evil spirits.

She herself was in as good a humour as anyone could remember having seen her. She hedgehogged back and forth, humming snatches from *The Sound of Music*, and occasionally remarking under her breath, "Oh well – all part of life, I s'pose," and "You can't get blacker than black."

When she came out with this latter remark for about the fourth time, Mr Bagthorpe burst out:

"Hell's bells, what's she *mean*, blacker than black!"

"I don't believe I have heard that expression before," Mrs Bagthorpe told her, with a warning frown at her husband. "How interesting and unusual."

58

"It's what my ma used to say," Mrs Fosdyke confided. "'Ad lots of sayings, my ma did."

The Bagthorpes stared. No one had, until this moment, ever thought of Mrs Fosdyke as having a mother. For that matter, it was difficult to think of her as ever having been a child. She fell into the category of those beings who seem to have come into the world fully fledged, just as they are.

"You never hear of *witches* having mothers," Jack thought, "or Donald Duck. *Or* being children."

The reason for Mrs Fosdyke's present good humour soon became clear.

"We shall hold our séance properly, this time," Mr Bagthorpe told everybody. "I am sick of bungling and bodging. We shall sit down in total darkness at eleven forty-five, which will give us a quarter of an hour to Call Up the Spirits before midnight."

"You can't expect spirits to be punctual," Tess told him. "They're entirely autonomous, and can't be evoked to order."

"I expect I shall be back by then," said Mrs Fosdyke.

"Back?" echoed Mrs Bagthorpe. "Why – where are you going, Mrs Fosdyke, dear?"

Not, she fervently hoped, to book her ticket back to England.

"I'm meeting my friends," replied Mrs Fosdyke complacently. "We're 'aving a drink in The Welsh 'Arp. Though what Welsh Guinness'll turn out to be like, I don't know."

Mr Bagthorpe began to choke. His offspring, who had heard of Mrs Fosdyke's treachery from Rosie, looked at her with cold dislike.

"I—I didn't know you had any friends here," Mrs Bagthorpe said.

"I've made some," Mrs Fosdyke informed her. "I *always* make friends on 'oliday. It's what 'olidays is for, partly. There's Mavis Evans, and there's Megan Jones, that 'elps in the shop. Ever so nice they are."

At the name of Jones all present stiffened. Despite their having learned earlier that there were at least thirty-six thousand of them in the district, this sounded distinctly ominous.

"How very nice that you have already made yourself a social life," said Mrs Bagthorpe weakly. Her husband was clenching and unclenching his fists.

"I'll get my garlic put out, and my pentagon drawn before I go," continued Mrs Fosdyke happily. "I was wondering if you'd fetch me in the car, Mrs Bagthorpe? I didn't think you'd want me walking back in the dark."

"Oh—oh yes, of course! And I'll take you there, too."

The looks of dislike intensified. Not only was Mrs Fosdyke laying claim to having had a mother, she was now expecting to be ferried back and forth to social engagements. The meal over, she left the others to do the washing up, and trotted off upstairs to get ready. She then reappeared in peach crimplene, looking uncommonly smug.

"Judas Carrot!" muttered Jack, as she was chauffeured off by Mrs Bagthorpe.

"I'm going to start on that boiler while she's out of the way," William said. "If she's going to sell us down the river, she can bake us some cakes while she's at it."

Tess had completed setting up her ghost-detecting equipment, and was now in a sulk about the lack of washing facilities.

"I haven't had a bath for two days!" she wailed. "I must smell horrible!"

"Of *course* you don't, darling!" cried Mrs Bagthorpe, who had just returned. She had to reassure Tess about this a lot, even at home, where she often took two baths a day. She had fortunately won large quantities of toilet preparations during the Competition Entering period, but was still convinced that she smelt.

"All adolescent girls go through this phase," Mrs Bagthorpe continued. "They all think they smell."

"I daresay they do," replied Tess, uncomforted, "but in my case, it's true."

"It most certainly is," William said.

"There!" cried Tess. "I told you!"

"Don't be silly, William," his mother told him.

"If anyone smells, it's you," Jack put in.

A row then set up as to who smelt and who didn't, but at the end of the day it was agreed by all that given the primitive washing arrangements at Ty Cilion Duon, there was a fair chance that they would all end up smelling quite strongly.

"We'll be as high as kites," William said.

"*We* shall have to make some friends in the village, like Fozzy," Tess said. "Then we can go to their houses for baths."

No one commented. They were all well aware that they had not so far made a very good impression on the inhabitants of Llosilli.

"*If* anyone'll even speak to us," Tess went on

61

bitterly. "It's all that Daisy's fault. *I* know what I'll do! I'll go up to *their* place and have a bath. I can use Daisy's bathroom. I expect Uncle Parker's paying for it, even if she doesn't use it."

She went off to fetch her toilet things, and departed.

"We'll have bags of hot water once I've got this thing cleaned up," William said.

He sounded considerably more optimistic than he felt. The interior of the boiler, once he had prised open the rusted door, looked like the mouth of hell. William was a wizard at the drums, tennis and electronics, but plumbing had never been a String to his Bow. Indeed, none of the Bagthorpes were very strong on Do It Yourself. Such mundane activities as hammering in nails or mending leaking taps had never appealed. No one had ever won a Nobel Prize knocking in nails.

William did not, to begin with, know which end of the range was the oven, and which the boiler. Both looked equally cavernous and begrimed.

"I'll clean 'em both, and sort it out later," he decided.

It was a pity that he did not notice at this stage that the boiler was not in fact connected up to anything, even a chimney. It had been bought as scrap by Mr Jones, who intended to sell when the price was right.

Within an hour the range was marginally cleaner, the kitchen was covered by a thick layer of soot and rust, and William resembled a miner just up from the pit. Unfortunately, no one had been present to witness, and put a stop to, his furious activities.

Rose was playing her violin, Mrs Bagthorpe was writing letters, Grandma practising Self-Hypnosis and

Mr Bagthorpe in his study, presumably Drawing Himself Up.

Jack, who had been out with Zero exploring the grounds, was first to come in.

"Good grief!" he exclaimed. He stopped dead, watching Zero pad over the floor leaving a clear set of prints like tracks in snow.

"A-shoo!" The air was still full of a fine drizzle of smuts.

William straightened up. He glowered. The whites of his eyes gleamed in his blackened face.

"Don't *you* start," he said bad-temperedly. "It's bad enough with Father pretending to sneeze the whole time."

"I'm—shoo—not pretending!" Jack protested.

Mrs Bagthorpe then entered.

"Oh, great heavens, whatever—ashoo!" she cried. Her eyes roamed wildly over the blackened scene.

63

"Oh William!" she wailed. "How *could* you? What shall we do? Whatever—oh, whatever will Mrs Fosdyke say?"

Nobody even attempted to answer this. Rosie appeared behind her.

"What's going on?" she demanded. "What—a-shoo!"

At this juncture Tess, newly bathed and deliciously scented, skipped in.

"Oh it was bliss!" she cried. "Utter heaven! There's a sunken bath, everybody, and—"

She stopped dead. Her eyes widened with horror and disbelief. Next minute, she was back in the hall.

"You beast!" she screamed. "You've done it on purpose, just because you knew I was having a bath!"

She ran off upstairs, sobbing. The culture shock of coming straight from the Parkers' elegant five star brand of civilization to the privations of her own holiday home was evidently too much for her. Mr Bagthorpe then inevitably emerged. Any Drawing Up that had been achieved was rapidly Undrawn. He shook his head for a long time, taking in the scene. "Am I in Purgatory?" he asked. "Or am I in Hell?"

This inquiry sounded quite genuine.

"Fat lot of thanks I get!" said William bitterly. "There's none of *you* would've tackled the filthy brute, though I expect you'll all scoff the cakes when they get baked. I'm off up to Uncle Park's for a shower."

"But, William," protested his mother, "you can't possibly go up to the castle in that state!"

"I can," he replied, "and I will. And with any luck I might even get a meal."

He departed, and a minute or so later made his way down the drive, looking like a miner strayed from the Rhondda.

"Oh dear!" said Mrs Bagthorpe helplessly. "It will be dreadfully embarrassing for poor Russell and Celia. Whatever will the other guests think?"

"Do not waste your sympathy on Russell and Celia," her husband told her. "They are by now immune to embarrassment. Anyone who goes through the world with that unholy infant and her goat in tow is beyond embarrassment. For all we know, the castle is already on fire."

"Oh that's *right*!" cried Rosie passionately. "Turn everything round so's it's all poor little Daisy's fault! *William*'s made all this muck. And I'm not cleaning it up, so there! I'm damn and blast not!"

"Rosie!" murmured Mrs Bagthorpe, shocked.

Grandma, scenting a Row, appeared in the doorway.

"There is nothing the matter, I hope?" she inquired insincerely.

No one replied.

"I have been practising Self-Hypnosis," she continued. "Unfortunately, this requires conditions of deep peace and harmony, if it is to be successful. There *is* no deep peace and harmony in this household."

No one troubled to respond to this statement of the obvious.

"Dear Tess tells me that there is a splendid sunken bath at the castle," she continued. "And we have an open invitation to use it. Perhaps you will be good enough to run me up there, Henry?"

"William's already *in* the bath," Jack pointed out.

65

"I shall talk with darling Daisy while I wait for it to become vacant," she said. "She and I have much to discuss."

"I will take you, Mother," said Mrs Bagthorpe hastily. "Jack dear – and Henry, *do* make some effort to clean up while we are gone."

"I shall do no such thing," replied Mr Bagthorpe. "As a matter of fact, the state this kitchen is in exactly matches my own mood. And I do not see why a constant procession of my relatives has to go kowtowing up to that capitalist-infested gin palace up the road for baths. You may inform Russell from me that I shall not avail myself of this facility. Tell him to sink in his own bath."

He followed his wife and mother out into the drive and shouted similar messages of goodwill after them as they drove off.

"Though there is one thing," he told the others on his return. "I should not think that the appearance of William up there has done Russell's reputation much good. He resembled the demon king. He would certainly not have passed for a holder of American Express. Ha!"

"Uncle Park's got a *gold* American Express card," Rosie piped up tactlessly. "He showed it to me."

"Be quiet!" Mr Bagthorpe snapped. "And be thankful that *you* are not being brought up in such an atmosphere of decadent luxuriousness."

"We certainly aren't," Jack agreed warmly.

He wondered whether the bleakness of their present surrounds was really improving their characters, as his father claimed. He was certainly not aware of it, though perhaps, he reflected, character-building was an undetectable process. On the other hand, nobody's temper seemed to be improving. It was not making anybody patient and resigned. The Bagthorpes were first and last tireless fighters against the pricks. For them, resignation would begin only with the grave.

Mr Bagthorpe went slamming off to his makeshift study.

"*I'm* not cleaning up," said Rosie. She too stomped off. Jack began the search for a bucket and mop.

"I'm having *my* character strengthened more than anybody," he told himself, and was momentarily cheered by the thought, and wondered whether this could be counted as a String to his Bow, even if it were invisible. He doubted it. The Bagthorpes were not much interested in the invisible things of this world. (Except, at the moment, for ghosts. And even these would have to materialize if they were to count for anything.)

It was not easy cleaning up with cold water. When he had finished the floor Jack leaned on his mop and surveyed the result. This was distinctly streaky. It certainly did not look like a TV advert for a power cleanser. Mrs Bagthorpe then returned and herself feverishly rolled up her sleeves for the attack. She was worried that having had a taste of civilization and its comforts at The Welsh Harp, Mrs Fosdyke would on her return take one look and announce her immediate return to England. She confided this fear to Jack.

"So we must make it look more like home," she told him.

"That'll be the day," he said. "Have they got the goat back?"

"Oh—would you believe!" She clapped a hand to her mouth. "Do you know, I quite forgot to ask. How dreadful of me!"

"I don't see why," Jack said. "We've all got plenty on our plates without asking about goats."

"Celia was in raptures," she told him. "She says that she wishes to dwell in Wales for ever. Live, I mean."

"I expect she said dwell," Jack said. "Poor old Uncle Park."

A thought struck him.

"Where's William?" he demanded. "Why didn't he come back down with you? *I* know why. He makes all this muck, and then leaves everyone else to clear it up."

"He—he has been invited to stay for a meal," Mrs Bagthorpe informed him. "He is, after all, a growing boy."

"So am I," Jack reminded her. "When I've got time."

By ten o'clock the kitchen was more or less restored to its original state. Jack lit his camping stove and made a cup of tea. He took a cup each to Mr Bagthorpe and Grandpa. He and Mrs Bagthorpe had just sat down with theirs when William returned.

"That meal," he said with satisfaction, "was something else again!"

"You can spare us the details," Jack told him. "Shall you and me go up there for a bath?" he asked his mother.

"It's rather late," she replied, "and by now I expect little Daisy is settling down to sleep."

Here she was very wide of the mark. The words had hardly died on her lips when they heard the screech of tyres in the drive.

"Ah, that will be Russell bringing Mother home," she said.

Next moment Daisy Parker, looking as chipper as ever, came prancing in. She was, admittedly, minus the goat, but nevertheless had an air of boundless energy that boded ill, especially at that hour of the night. Aunt Celia always said that Daisy needed very little sleep. This she attributed to an over-powerful brain, but the Bagthorpes had their own theories — none of them flattering.

"Hello, Daisy," said Jack. "Where's the goat?"

"Oh, he feeding on verdant pashers," she informed him happily. This was clearly a direct quote from Aunt Celia. "He grazing pashers green."

"It is to be hoped that that is *all* he is doing," said Mr Bagthorpe grimly. He had heard Uncle Parker's car draw up and emerged looking for a Row. "Why, Russell, in the name of all that is wonderful, have you brought your offspring back down here? I have told you, I have told you a thousand times, that she is *persona non grata*." He paused. "As you are yourself," he added.

Grandma then wafted in, deliciously scented.

"Darling Daisy has come to spend the night," she announced.

"She has *what*?" demanded Mr Bagthorpe. "Russell, you are deranged."

"Surely dear Celia will not wish Daisy to be present at a séance?" interposed Mrs Bagthorpe. "Surely. . . ?"

"Celia is at present in a state of euphoria," Uncle Parker explained.

"He means manic," Mr Bagthorpe told them.

"She feels that the air is filled with ancestral voices calling," Uncle Parker continued. "She feels that she has found her spiritual home."

He looked about him at their blank faces.

"Something like that," he concluded apologetically.

"And naturally she wishes Daisy to hear, and respond to, those same voices," Grandma said. "Daisy is a vessel of pure poetry."

Tess and Rosie appeared, forestalling a debate about this which would doubtless have been heated, if not bloody.

"Hurray, it's Daisy!" cried Rosie. "Ace! Where's Billy Goat Gruff?"

"I expect," said William, "that by now he's been eaten by a dragon."

"No!" squealed Daisy. "No no no!"

"Wicked boy!" Grandma reproved in ringing tones. "Corrupter of innocence!"

"He's still on the loose," Jack told Rosie. "And still chewing his way through everything."

Daisy was not satisfied by this blunt paraphrase.

"He not. He feeding on verdant pashers," she insisted. "An' I come to stop and catch ghosties."

"Ace!" Rosie, at least, was delighted. "You can sleep in my bed with me, after. Did you know this house had Black Corners, Daisy?"

"If it hadn't before, it has now," Mr Bagthorpe said. "Personally, I believe the whole world to be one almighty big Black Corner. As far as I'm concerned, the riddle of the universe is now solved. It all fits. It—"

He ranted on. Nobody paid the slightest attention. They had, after all, heard most of it before. Most of Mr Bagthorpe's favourite phrases suffered from over-frequent repetition. They tended to recur – like onions (or garlic).

Six

Meanwhile, Mrs Fosdyke was finding The Welsh Harp a veritable home from home. Even the Guinness tasted exactly the same as that in The Fiddler's Arms. She sat in a corner with her two new friends, happily shopping the Bagthorpes left and right.

"What kind of people *are* they, Mrs Fosdyke?" inquired Mrs Evans.

"Call me Gladys," responded Mrs Fosdyke cordially. "Oooh, you couldn't *describe* 'em, never in an 'undred years. If you 'ad to put it in a nutshell, though, the nearest you could come would be to say mad."

"Mad?" echoed Mrs Jones, alarmed.

"Mad as 'atters," nodded Mrs Fosdyke. "All of 'em. But especially '*im*. You'd never believe the life I live, Mrs Jones."

"Call me Megan," urged her new friend. "Well off, are they?"

"Rich as Croesus," confirmed Mrs Fosdyke. "Their 'ouse back at 'ome is full of hairlooms. Mind you, the rate they smash things and burn 'em down, it soon won't be."

"Smash?" echoed Mrs Jones. "Burn?"

"Oooh, regular as clockwork," Mrs Fosdyke told

them. "The Fire Brigade is hardly never off the doorstep."

By now other conversation in the room had died away and all present sat listening unashamedly to Mrs Fosdyke's pronouncements. As the evening wore on the pub filled up with locals, and Mrs Fosdyke held court in her corner, graciously accepting Guinnesses from her new acquaintances. (These were offered not so much in a spirit of generosity as in the hopes that they would loosen her tongue.)

The village was still in a state of alert on account of Billy Goat Gruff being still on the loose.

"We're going round in pairs, see," Mrs Evans told her. "No one to walk alone."

"You want to do," nodded Mrs Fosdyke. "That goat'd kill people, if it got the chance. *And* it drinks."

"Drinks?" prompted Mrs Jones, puzzled.

"Whisky," Mrs Fosdyke told her. "Gets drunk as a lord and rams everything in sight."

She made it sound like an everyday occurrence. By now she had herself imbibed rather more stout than she was accustomed to, and all attempts at accuracy had flown out of the window.

"Them Parkers is mad as well," she told everybody. "Them that's stopping up at the castle, and 'im screeching about in that red car. And as for that child!" She paused and shuddered expressively. "There's times when I think she's 'ardly even 'uman. Setting fire to everything and flooding it, writing on walls, everlasting digging graves . . ."

"Graves?" interrupted Mrs Evans incredulously.

"Graves," affirmed Mrs Fosdyke. "Got a regular cemetery set up, she 'as, in a corner of the garden.

Blasphemy, o' course, and I told Mrs Bagthorpe as much. 'It's a wonder that Daisy Parker ain't struck by a thunderbolt from 'eaven,' I told her."

She patently regretted that this had not been the case, and thought the Almighty negligent in this respect.

"You want to tell your police force to get her locked up, next chance they get," she continued. "And then sent off for one of them short sharp shocks. Or p'raps a *long* sharp shock."

And so on, and on. So deeply was Mrs Fosdyke into her theme of the general madness and degeneracy of the entire Bagthorpe clan that she scarcely noticed the time. She did not even notice when the barman called "Last orders, please!"

It was only when Mrs Evans reluctantly said that she must be going now, on account of her husband, who was in bed with a slipped disc and probably waiting for his cocoa, that Mrs Fosdyke realized that the evening was at an end.

"It's been *ever* so interesting, Gladys," her new friends assured her warmly. "We'll 'ave to meet regular, while you're here."

"It's certainly took me out of meself," Mrs Fosdyke told them.

This was, by now, quite literally the case. She had imbibed so much stout that she had only the foggiest notion of where she was, or how she was to get home – if Ty Cilion Duon could be so described. She got up, clutching her handbag, and hooked her arm into that of Mrs Jones – more as a means of steadying herself than as a gesture of friendship. The three ladies wove their way to the door and out into the night.

Mrs Fosdyke, who had the vague impression that she had spent the evening in The Fiddler's Arms, looked about her for the route home, and could not see it.

"What's them 'umps?" she demanded of her companions—meaning the mountains. They, looking vainly about them for camels, were naturally non-plussed.

Meanwhile, up at Ty Cilion Duon, the Bagthorpes had clean forgotten about Mrs Fosdyke. They had mislaid her in much the same way as they had earlier mislaid Grandpa. This was excusable, up to a point. They were not used to having her about in the evenings. At Unicorn House she usually scuttled off with relief at five or six o'clock, and they, with equal relief, watched her go. A round-the-clock Mrs Fosdyke was outside their experience.

Also, it could be pleaded in mitigation that they were engaged in an almighty Row. This was specifically about whether or not Daisy should be allowed to spend the night at Ty Cilion Duon, but as always with Bagthorpian Rows, it had led to all kinds of ramifications and the dredging up of endless past grievances. Mrs Fosdyke, had she been present, would herself have thoroughly enjoyed it, and found plenty of chances of putting in her own oar. She might even have swayed the issue in favour of Daisy's going back up to the castle.

As it was, Grandma, as usual, won the day. (She was supported by Rosie, of course, and by Uncle Parker himself, but it was she who really swung it.)

"We'll have a vote," Mr Bagthorpe suggested, confident that it would be a vote in his own favour.

"We shall do no such thing," returned Grandma coolly. "A vote, Henry, would merely be a pandering to the lowest instincts of all involved, especially yourself. Justice has nothing to do with votes. And in this case, of course, we are talking about Poetic Justice."

"That brat," replied Mr Bagthorpe, "has about as much to do with poetry as the moon has to do with green cheese."

"There!" cried Grandma triumphantly. "You have proved my point exactly!"

"Der moon *is* green cheese," squealed Daisy. "*An'* it's a ghostie gallyon, *an'* it come tumbling down into a dish of porridge!"

"Oh my God!" said Mr Bagthorpe wearily. "I give up."

"Right, then!" exclaimed Uncle Parker with alacrity, leaping to his feet. "That's settled. I'll be off, if you don't mind. Celia and myself are learning Welsh, and wish to get stuck straight in."

"Nobody has ever understood a single word of any *English* poetry Celia has written," rejoined Mr Bagthorpe. "And so I suppose that little will change when she launches into the Welsh tongue."

By now Uncle Parker was at the door, making good his getaway.

"There is one thing certain, Henry," he remarked over his shoulder, "*you* will never sit in a Bardic Chair."

Before Mr Bagthorpe had time to come up with a suitably cutting retort, Uncle Parker was out in the drive, in his car, firing his own retort.

So it was that barely a minute later Uncle Parker glimpsed a pedestrian in his headlights and was forced to swerve violently, braking hard. He was, as usual, driving much too fast and would, as Mr Bagthorpe later pointed out, undoubtedly have faced a charge of manslaughter had he not managed to avoid hitting Mrs Fosdyke.

"And what a pity that you *did*," he added. "It would have killed two birds with one stone, and improved the quality of my own life beyond measure."

Shaken as he was Uncle Parker had nonetheless caught a fractional glimpse of the figure in his headlights and was sure that, against all probability, it had been that of Mrs Fosdyke. No one had mentioned to him that she had gone out for a social evening, and he had not really missed her presence back at the house.

"Better check," he thought. "But whatever would the old bat be doing rambling around the countryside at this hour?"

Accordingly he slammed his gear into reverse and shot backwards up the road only marginally slower than he had come down it.

"Good grief!" he exclaimed. "It *is* her!"

There, sitting forlornly on the bank at the roadside, was Mrs Fosdyke, her hat tilted over one eye and the contents of her handbag scattered about her. She blinked owlishly in the dazzling headlights.

Uncle Parker leapt out and gallantly started picking up the trail of handkerchiefs, indigestion pills, biros and so forth.

"Great Scott, Mrs F.," he greeted her. "What's up? Are you all right?"

She seemed not to hear him.

"I can't think 'ow I come here," she said plaintively, more or less to herself. "The 'ole world's

77

changed. Where's all the 'ouses gone? Where's *my* 'ouse?"

"Shock," thought Uncle Parker, who did not know about the earlier intake of Guinness.

"Come along, now, Mrs F.," he urged, helping her to her feet. "You've had a bit of a turn. You really ought to wear fluorescent clothing, you know, if you're going to walk all over the road at night. It's people like you who cause all the accidents. Thank God my reflexes are first class."

The dazed Mrs Fosdyke meekly allowed herself to be helped into the passenger seat of Uncle Parker's car. This in itself was a measure of her disorientation. Normally, wild horses could not have induced her to do such a thing. She regarded getting into Uncle Parker's car as tantamount to committing suicide, and said as much, frequently.

Uncle Parker swung his car round and raced back to Ty Cilion Duon. There he deposited his passenger at the front door.

"I shan't come in," he told her. "Got to dash. Have a nice cup of hot sweet tea. Cheers!"

Mrs Fosdyke stood staring after his taillights. She

shook her head long and hard. She then opened the door and went in. She looked at the tumbled pile of objects still blocking the hall.

"'Oliday," she muttered vaguely. "I'm on 'oliday."

As she entered the kitchen Mrs Bagthorpe clapped a hand to her mouth and emitted a shriek. She went quite white.

"Oh dear!" she cried. "Oh dear, how *dreadful*! How absolutely unforgivable! Oh Mrs Fosdyke, how will you ever forgive me? Oh, it is dreadful! Oh, I feel totally –"

"Oh, stop *rambling*, Laura," said Mr Bagthorpe irritably. "All you did was forget to pick her up. Most natural thing in the world, if you ask me."

"Do come along, Mrs Fosdyke, dear, and sit down," Mrs Bagthorpe continued. "Jack, dear, pull up that deckchair. And put the kettle on. Oh, whatever has happened – look at your beautiful suit, all covered in mud and grass! Have you had an accident? Have you – oh, tell me that you have not been assaulted!"

Mrs Fosdyke sank into the proffered deckchair and sat quite peacefully, holding her handbag to her. She seemed to have reverted to the trance-like state brought on by the shock of first seeing the kitchen.

"I've 'ad ever such a nice evening," she informed the room at large. She sat there, smiling foolishly. The Bagthorpes gaped. Mrs Fosdyke practically never smiled.

"Make the tea, quick, Jack!" Mrs Bagthorpe commanded. "And put three heaped spoonfuls of sugar in. No, four."

"Make it five," advised her husband. "An overdose." Then, with uncanny accuracy, "If you ask me, she's been winged by Russell, on the road."

"Oh, how can you say such a thing!" cried his wife. "Mrs Fosdyke, tell us, were you struck by a car, or a bicycle, perhaps?"

"I seen these enormous big lights like great yellow eyes," said Mrs Fosdyke dreamily. "And then I 'ad a little sit down. Me legs felt funny, and me 'ead." She paused. "I still feel ever so far away," she confessed —and smiled again.

"Look," said Mr Bagthorpe, "it's already gone eleven o'clock and we've a deadly serious séance on hand. I will not have it sabotaged. Why doesn't she take her funny legs and head off to bed, and leave the rest of us to it?"

"Oooh, o' course!" said Mrs Fosdyke. "I'd clear forgot about all them ghosts and spirits and were-wolves. Do you know, I don't much care *what* I see, tonight."

"Hell's *bells*!" muttered Mr Bagthorpe under his breath. "The woman's clean lost her marbles."

"Mrs Fosdyke has every right to attend the séance, Henry," Grandma told him. "Indeed, she appears to know more about the whole matter than you do yourself. It would not at all surprise me if she were a sensitive, a psychic."

"Sensitive?" echoed Mr Bagthorpe. "*Sensitive?* Like Lady Macbeth, she is! Like Lucrezia Borgia, like—"

"Uncle Bag," piped up Daisy, "can we put the lights off? Ghosties like it dark."

"How wise the child is," murmured Grandma.

Mrs Fosdyke's glance rested thoughtfully for a moment on Daisy, then passed on. She made no comment. Her usual reaction to Daisy was that of a bull to the proverbial red rag.

"She *has* gone bananas," Jack thought. "Must have."

"We cannot sit about prattling for the next hour," Mr Bagthorpe said. "We will put out the lights and sit in total silence. That will allow those of us who *are* sensitive to Draw Ourselves Up."

"Are you sure you feel up to it, Mrs Fosdyke?" Mrs Bagthorpe inquired nervously.

"Oooh, *ever* so sure," responded Mrs Fosdyke happily. "Fair looking forward to it, I am. It'll be as good as a film."

"Would you perhaps like a bulb of garlic to hold?" persisted Mrs Bagthorpe.

"Oh, well, yes, you could just 'and me one of them," Mrs Fosdyke agreed graciously, though she really did not seem to care way or the other.

"I, too, will have one," said Grandma. "And one for Daisy, please. In fact, for all of us who are especially sensitive."

Her son shot her a murderous glare.

"I shall sit with Little Tommy on my lap," she continued. "He, too, is a sensitive. It may well be that he will witness entities invisible to the rest of us."

"And Zero," put in Jack jealously. "*He'll* know when something comes, all right. Where's Grandpa?"

"He has gone to bed," Grandma told him. "He has informed me that he is not interested in the spirit world. He has always been hopelessly prosaic. Jack, dear, pass me my Bible and then put out the lights."

Mrs Bagthorpe was still distributing the garlic. Rosie requested that she, too, should have some. Tess and

William were busy setting up their respective equipment. The former had wired herself up to a device to measure her galvanic skin-response, and the latter intended to tape anything a visiting spirit might say.

"Remember," he told everybody, "even if *we* do not hear anything, the tape may well pick up a disembodied voice."

"It won't," said Rosie in a quaky voice. "I know it won't."

The company assembled themselves in a circle and the lights were put out. An immediate silence fell. All of them were hoping that once their eyes adjusted they would be able to see at least a little—enough, at any rate, to make a break for the door if anything emerged from a Black Corner. This was not the case. For all they could make out, they might as well have been sitting in a coal-hole.

"You hold my hand," Jack heard Rosie whisper — presumably to Daisy.

The silence went on and on. It was probably the longest recorded silence ever to occur among Bagthorpes. It began to seem to Jack that already he could sense cold, moving presences.

"I hope one of them's the Bearded Man Carrying a Candle," he thought. "Then at least I'll be able to see Zero's fur stand up on end."

No sooner had this thought occurred to him than he felt Zero stiffen under his hand. There came a low, soft growl. Jack felt the nape of his neck creep. He strained into the darkness, but could see nothing. Again Zero growled.

"W-what's the matter with Z-Zero?" quavered Rosie.

"Sshh!" came angry hisses from all sides. By now Jack had forgotten where everyone was sitting. The silence was total and tense. It was the kind of silence you get when a lot of people are holding their breaths. Then, quite close to Jack himself, came an unmistakable slithering sound, a soft scuffle.

"Ooooh!" moaned poor Rosie.

"Ssshh!" came the chorus of hisses again.

Silence.

"Are the spirits with us tonight?"

Everyone jumped as Mr Bagthorpe's sepulchral tones came out of the blackness.

He paused, presumably to give any spirits present the chance to declare themselves, then repeated the inquiry, twice more.

At this point Daisy, disappointed by the lack of action, herself came up with an invitation.

"Ghosties ghosties come to play!" she piped. "Ghosties ghosties come to play!"

"Shut *up*!" came Mr Bagthorpe's furious voice through his invisible clenched teeth.

There was another long silence. Then, faintly but unmistakably, there came the sound of breathing, deep and heavy. In . . . out . . . in . . . out . . . a regular, sighing rhythm.

"Help!" Jack thought. "It's definitely not Grandma doing her Breathing, or Mother. It's disembodied Breathing!"

He did not remember there being a Disembodied Breather in Mr Bagthorpe's list of phantoms, but supposed it must have come out of one of the many Black Corners.

They all sat transfixed. The smell of garlic

intensified. Gradually the breathing deepened. Then came the soft rattling of a snore. Mrs Fosdyke had dropped off.

"It's that woman!" came Mr Bagthorpe's enraged whisper. "Give her a poke, whoever's near her. Stop her!"

Next minute there was an almighty clatter and screech, followed by high-pitched shrieks from practically everyone present. Their nerves, strained to snapping point, had finally snapped. People were stumbling about in the dark and screaming when they touched another person. Jack groped for the light and turned it on.

The ghost-spotters were in total disarray. This applied particularly to Mrs Fosdyke, who was lying on her back like a beached turtle amid her collapsed deckchair, and crying:

"Oooh, oooh, *now* what's 'appened? Where am I? Where am I?"

William, obeying his father's instruction to give Mrs Fosdyke a dig to stop her snoring, had in the darkness inadvertently unhinged her deckchair instead.

Tess was screaming, "It's up! The reading's up — there was something there! Oh—*look* where you're going, can't you!"

Grandma was clutching her Bible so hard that her knuckles were white. Rosie was sobbing, "I want to go home, I want to go home!" while Daisy attempted to comfort her.

"Don't cry, Rosie," she begged. "*I* look after you, me an' Arry Awk! We won't let the ghosties get you!"

She seemed the calmest person present. Jack sup-

posed that this was because she was already well accustomed to the presence of an invisible entity in the shape of Arry Awk.

"I must make some hot sweet tea!" cried Mrs Bagthorpe urgently.

"Personally," said her husband, "I'll settle for Scotch!" He made for the door, and turned. "And tomorrow," he added, "we shall all go home!"

The door slammed behind him. The rest stared after him, each trying in his or her own way to take in this astonishing volte-face. Mr Bagthorpe was always changing his position to suit his own convenience – no one, for instance, knew what his politics (if any) were, from one day to the next. But this was easily the most drastic turnaround anyone could remember. It was Mrs Bagthorpe who finally broke the silence.

"Never mind!" she cried. "Let us see what the morrow brings!"

They stared at her in disgust. She sounded exactly like Aunt Celia. They morosely downed their hot sweet tea and went to bed, followed by the thick, pungent smell of crushed garlic.

Seven

Next morning Mr Bagthorpe did not appear at breakfast. Everyone assumed that he was holed up somewhere, sulking and licking his wounds. His absence gave them the chance to discuss his announcement of the previous night.

"It could be that he did not mean it at all," said Mrs Bagthorpe wisely.

"Let's go straight away, today," begged Rosie. "Did you hear that horrible slithering and scraping? Ugh!"

"Don't worry, Rosie," Jack told her. He had now had time to think about this. "It must've been Little Tommy. We didn't see him, but Zero did. He growled."

"Little Tommy was on Grandma's lap," William pointed out.

"Was he?" Tess asked. "Or did he jump off?"

"I do not remember," said Grandma untruthfully. She did, of course. The cat *had* left her lap, quite soon after the lights went out. It did not, however, suit her book to say so. She liked to have everyone on the hop, and by now most of the Bagthorpes were very jumpy indeed.

"It was all Fozzy's fault," said Tess bitterly. Her wires and meters had been disconnected and trampled upon during the mêlée following the collapse of Mrs Fosdyke's deckchair. She was able to make this accusation in the absence of Mrs Fosdyke herself, who was still upstairs, slumbering peacefully.

"Let us put the whole thing behind us," said Mrs Bagthorpe sensibly. Her gift for Positive Thinking was such that she would probably make exactly the same suggestion on the morning following a nuclear holocaust.

"I have thought of a lovely treat for us all today," she continued brightly.

Her offspring looked at her without enthusiasm. Her idea of a treat and their own rarely coincided.

"Straight after breakfast," she said, "we shall set off for a day out. We shall go to a perfectly splendid country auction that I have seen advertised."

"How will we, Mother?" inquired William. "We have only one car. And there were ten of us, at the last count."

"Oh yes. Oh dear!" Mrs Bagthorpe's Positive Thinking was not always in accordance with Clear Thinking.

"I'm not going anyway," Rosie said. "Or Daisy. We're going on a Dragon Quest."

"How enterprising!" cried her mother. "But I cannot possibly allow the two of you to stay here alone. You are far too young."

"Grandpa'll be here," Daisy pointed out.

"And me," said William.

"And me," said Tess.

"Then seating arrangements in the car will work

out splendidly," said Mrs Bagthorpe. "Those of you who stay here will have a chance to practise your instruments. We do not of course yet know whether Mrs Fosdyke will go to the sale, but I think it likely. She is anxious to acquire a draining board."

"A *what*?"

It was Mr Bagthorpe who had just entered, looking extremely hollow-eyed and ill-tempered. What the others did not know was that he had, once everyone else had gone to bed, carried on the séance single-handed. He genuinely did believe himself to be sensitive, and had spent half the night invoking phantoms. Being so obsessive by nature he had given up only as dawn broke. He had been tempted to sleep through most of the day, to avoid the miseries of existence alongside his family, but had remembered the auction. His urgent need of a desk had prompted him to set his alarm. He had had less than four hours' sleep.

"A draining board," repeated Mrs Bagthorpe, as her husband cast vainly round for somewhere to sit.

"On which to beat out everlasting tattoos with pots and pans," rejoined Mr Bagthorpe. "Do they, by any chance, make draining boards in foam rubber?"

"I am myself greatly looking forward to the auction," Grandma said. "There may be all kinds of attractive pieces for the time when Alfred and I have a home of our own."

"That," said Mr Bagthorpe bitterly, "will be the day. And you already have enough stuff in store to furnish Blenheim Palace."

This was, of course, an exaggeration, but did contain a grain of truth. Grandma and Grandpa had moved into Unicorn House over ten years previously on only a temporary basis.

"We shall not impose on your hospitality for long, Henry," Grandma had told her son. She had brought with her certain treasured possessions, and put all the other furniture in store.

From time to time over the years she would speak wistfully of the day when she and Grandpa could settle into their own home.

"Oh, what blessed peace there will be," she would sigh.

No one was fooled by this. If there was one thing Grandma could not stand, it was peace.

"If ever she gets it," Mr Bagthorpe would say, "the shock to her system will kill her."

At this point dragging footsteps were heard echoing on the stairs. So slow and slithering were they that Rosie, as jumpiest of the family, whispered, "Could it be a *daytime* ghost?"

It was, in fact, Mrs Fosdyke, descending the stairs with all the verve and speed of a glacier. She had awoken with a violent headache and in a dazed state. She honestly could not think where she was, and was coming down in order to find out. She appeared in the doorway, pop-eyed and swaying, and Mrs Bagthorpe hastily jumped up and offered her a deckchair. This must have stirred some vague recollection, because Mrs Fosdyke shook her head, even though doing so made her eyes feel like marbles.

"I ain't sitting in one of them," she announced. "Not ever again. Not even on the beach."

"Good!" said Mr Bagthorpe. "Thanks, Laura!" — and sat in it himself.

Life at Ty Cilion Duon involved, amongst other things, a constant game of Musical Chairs. Three unfortunates were always left standing, or sitting on the floor.

"Oooh, you were *funny* las' night, Mrs Fozzy!" squealed Daisy, bright-eyed and bushy-tailed as always, despite having gone to bed rather later than is usual for a five-year-old. She turned to the others.

"Wasn't Mrs Fozzy funny, all kicking about on the floor? Do it again, Mrs Fozzy, do it 'gain!"

Mrs Fosdyke gave her a look of open hatred.

"That means she's at least partly back to normal," Jack thought.

Mrs Bagthorpe saw the look, too, and made a mental note to have a firm word with Uncle Parker.

"I will tell him that Mrs Fosdyke is essential to our existence," she determined, "but that Daisy is not. I will telephone him straight away."

She got as far as the door, and then remembered that there was no telephone.

"Oh, this place really is quite dreadful," she thought Negatively. "No telephone, no hot water, no curtains, no cooker, no—"

She broke off this mental list abruptly.

"I am beginning to sound just like Mrs Fosdyke!"

Alarmed by this thought, she made an effort to do something Positive by writing a fairly strongly worded note to Uncle Parker. This she left in Rosie's charge, with instructions that it was to be handed to him immediately upon his arrival.

She then rounded up her party and they set off for the auction. Mr and Mrs Bagthorpe sat in the front of the car, Jack, Grandma and Mrs Fosdyke in the back.

Jack had left Zero in charge of Rosie, who said that she and Daisy would probably use him to sniff out dragons.

Mr Bagthorpe was disgusted by this.

"Why can't the dopey lump sniff out that accursed goat before it kills somebody?" he said. "Mutton-headed pudding-footed hound!"

The sale was being held in a large country house some thirty miles from Llosilli, so the journey was mercifully short. It was also quiet. Mr Bagthorpe did not feel that he had one single thing to say to Grandma or Mrs Fosdyke, and the latter was still mildly pole-axed anyway.

As soon as they arrived Mrs Bagthorpe went in search of catalogues.

"We have nearly an hour to look the items over before the sale begins," she told the others. "We can all mark off the items we are interested in, and perhaps make a note of what price we are prepared to go up to."

"There is no need for you to nanny us, Laura," Mr Bagthorpe told her rudely. "I am perfectly conversant with the procedure at auctions, thank you."

He announced his intention of going to "sort out" the auctioneer.

"I shall arrange a signal with him," he said, "so that he'll know I'm in the bidding, but no one else will. The raising of a newspaper, perhaps, or inclination of the eyebrow, or—"

"Or sneeze," suggested Jack helpfully.

"Don't be an idiot!" Mr Bagthorpe told him coldly, and went off in search of the auctioneer.

The others, now armed with catalogues, started their inspection of the various lots. Mrs Fosdyke scooted straight off into the Household Goods department. Mrs Bagthorpe hurried after her, to prevent her earmarking all kitchen equipment in sight. Jack himself quite enjoyed browsing about, though there was nothing he felt he wanted to buy.

Just before noon they settled themselves in their seats ready for the auction to commence. Mr Bagthorpe refused to sit with the others, and positioned himself some rows further back.

"What signal did you arrange with the auctioneer, dear?" his wife asked.

"Never you mind," he replied rudely.

This was a pity. Had he told her, she might have pointed out that a stifled yawn was not the most sensible of signals coming from one who had had less than four hours' sleep the previous night.

"Mrs Fosdyke and I have found some splendid formica-topped tables," Mrs Bagthorpe whispered to Jack. "They can be used as draining boards, and for all kinds of other purposes."

"Jolly good," Jack told her.

Grandma did not make any confidences about her own intended purchases. She sat wearing a look of quiet satisfaction that gave Jack, at least, misgivings. If Grandma was pleased, it was usually at someone else's expense.

By the end of the first hour Jack was beginning to wish he had stayed with the others at Ty Cilion Duon. After the novelty had worn off, the whole procedure was extremely tedious. Mrs Fosdyke was sitting between himself and Mrs Bagthorpe. Matters were not helped by her digging the latter in the ribs every few minutes, and hissing:

"Oooh, why don't you bid for that, Mrs Bagthorpe?" or "Oooh, that'd look a treat on the dresser!" and such. These objects were, presumably, ones that she would enjoy dusting.

Jack was just beginning to feel that he might nod off when he was aware that Grandma, on his other side, had stiffened, and was now perched on the edge of her seat, poised for action.

"What's she after?" He craned forward to see.

". . . in good working condition," the auctioneer was saying. "And with it, sets of recordings of various operas on the original 78 records. What about it, ladies and gentlemen? A rare chance, this. Forget about your stereo and your floppy discs. This kind of quality listening is a thing of the past. Now, who'll start me? Shall we say ten?"

"Yes!" said Grandma loudly, and stuck up her furled umbrella.

Jack thought he heard a groan from several rows behind them.

"Thank you, madam! Ten, then, who'll give me eleven . . . eleven . . ."

He did not waste much time trying to improve on Grandma's bid. She was evidently the only person in the room who wanted this lot. Later, the Bagthorpes would discover why.

Grandma sank back with a sigh of satisfaction. She was fairly certain that she had acquired something that would ensure there never again being a moment's peace in the Bagthorpe household.

After that things went quiet until towards the end

of the sale, when Household Goods were put up. Mrs Fosdyke did a good deal of muttering when items such as Hoovers, washing machines and fridges were offered. There was a lot of agitated whispering between herself and Mrs Bagthorpe that eventually caused heads to turn and frosty looks in their direction.

"Lot 318," the auctioneer announced. "Three formica-topped tables."

"That's them!" hissed Mrs Fosdyke, as the auctioneer enlarged on the merits of these extremely plain and unattractive items.

Mrs Bagthorpe used her rolled-up catalogue to indicate her bids. She just made ever so slight a movement with it – more, Jack thought, as if she were secretly bidding for a Dutch Master than three formica-topped tables.

The bidding started low, went up to twenty pounds, and after that advanced quite swiftly, in pounds. Jack suspected that someone sitting behind them was in competition with his mother. He craned round, but could see no sign of anyone bidding openly. Mr Bagthorpe just sat there, yawning non-stop.

When the bidding reached forty pounds Mrs Bagthorpe's gestures with her catalogue became increasingly nervous. On the one hand she had Mrs Fosdyke, hellbent on a draining board and some working surfaces, sitting right beside her. On the other, she had the distinct feeling that the tables under offer were not worth half that sum – quite apart from what Mr Bagthorpe would have to say about the matter.

"I shall have to stop at fifty," Jack heard her whisper desperately to Mrs Fosdyke.

She did. The three tables were knocked down at fifty-one pounds to the unknown bidder behind them. As they were carried off by the attendants, Jack saw the auctioneer crane forward and peer at them. He even ran a finger across one, evidently wondering whether he was losing his grip, and had mistaken marble, or onyx, for formica.

The Bagthorpe party then rose and made their way out.

"I must go and settle my account," said Grandma. "How delighted I am to have acquired such a bargain!"

Seen close up, the gramophone she had bought was clearly a very early model – possibly even the first ever. So antiquated did it look that it was hard to believe that it ran on electricity. It looked as if it pre-dated the discovery of electricity by decades. Beside it were stacks of 78 rpm records, most of them without sleeves. The scratches on the ones visible were of such an order that they might have been made by a determined assault with a screwdriver or attack by a vulture. Jack leaned over and read, "*La Bohême*."

"Is that an opera?" he asked. None of the Bagthorpes cared for opera, and no one had suspected until now that Grandma had any fondness for it.

"'Orrible foreign noises!" remarked Mrs Fosdyke dismissively. "And *now* what're we to do? No draining board, after all that! No tables, no working surfaces –"

"Did you manage to find a desk, dear?" Mrs Bagthorpe interrupted. "I don't believe one was offered, was it?"

"I have acquired a substitute," Mr Bagthorpe told her, "though at a price. Some lunatic was bidding against me. Who in God's name would pay fifty pounds for three such appalling objects beats me. However, a man as desperate for a desk as I am cannot afford to pick and choose. Ah – here they are!"

They followed his gaze.

"Them's *my* tables!" cried Mrs Fosdyke. "Look, Mrs Bagthorpe – 'e's *bought* 'em! And there we was, thinking we'd lost 'em!"

She scuttled over and ran her hands lovingly over their smooth surfaces. She turned to Mr Bagthorpe.

"Oooh, thanks *ever* so much, Mr Bagthorpe," she said. "Just think – a draining board!"

He looked at her with loathing.

"What is the woman burbling about?" he demanded. "I have never sat at a draining board to write, and do not intend to begin now."

"But – but Mrs Fosdyke and myself had earmarked these tables for use in the kitchen," faltered his wife. Light had dawned. Any minute now, when her

96

husband discovered who it was who had forced him up to such an exorbitant price for such awful objects, there would be the mother and father of a Row.

There was. For Mr Bagthorpe, too, light was dawning.

"Are you telling me," he demanded, "that it was *you* banging the damned things up a quid at a time against me?"

"But, Henry, how were we to know−?"

"You could have forced me up to hundred!" He was beginning to shout. "You could have forced me up to a *thousand*, Laura! Look at them−look at the flimsy, gimcrack things! A thousand pounds I could have paid for them, thanks to you!"

This, Jack thought, was probably true, given Mr Bagthorpe's obsessive nature.

"They'll be ever so useful," said Mrs Fosdyke happily. She was clearly not quite following what was being said.

"Never mind, Henry," said Mrs Bagthorpe. "You have your desk, and that is the main thing. And there will be two tables left for Mrs Fosdyke."

"There will *what*?" shouted her husband. "Do you seriously imagine I've forked out a sum like that to cut my own throat with a *draining board*?"

His metaphors were becoming mixed.

"I bought these tables, Laura, for use in my study. They are mine, mine, mine!"

He banged his fist on the nearest of the tables to emphasize his point. It swayed, teetered and two of its legs folded, bringing it, and Mr Bagthorpe, to the floor.

Extreme confusion followed. An attendant had already been sent to request that there should be less noise, because it was interfering with the auction next door.

"Faulty goods!" yelled Mr Bagthorpe, struggling to his feet. "I demand a refund! Where's the manager? Bring him here! I demand to see the manager!"

It took a very long time to quieten him down. Eventually he was made to understand that the sale was nearly at an end, and that then the auctioneer would himself deal with the matter. Witnesses of the scene appeared to be fairly solidly ranged against Mr Bagthorpe.

"The thump he gave that table, there's no wonder it collapsed," one woman said. "Anything would've collapsed. The Eiffel Tower would've."

"Have you seen my own purchases, Henry?" inquired Grandma, hoping to keep him on the boil. "And what a very large selection of operatic records."

"But why did you buy them, Mother?" asked Mrs Bagthorpe naively.

"She bought them," Mr Bagthorpe told her between gritted teeth, "with the express intention of driving us all out of our minds. She does not know *Die Fledermaus* from 'Baa Baa Black Sheep.' "

"I feel that they will raise the tone," remarked Grandma, "and improve the quality of all our lives. At present we seem to be living on a very low plane."

At this juncture the auctioneer himself mercifully appeared, or at least, it *seemed* merciful, at the time.

He cut the ground from under Mr Bagthorpe's feet

by conceding that the table must, indeed, have been faulty, and offering a reduction.

"Under normal circumstances, of course, I should not do so," he continued. "It is, after all, the responsibility of the intending purchaser to inspect the goods prior to the sale. Under these particular circumstances, however, I shall be happy to accommodate you."

"What circumstances?" demanded Mr Bagthorpe, somewhat deflated by so easy a victory.

The auctioneer smiled expansively.

"You are of course, sir, a very valued customer."

Mr Bagthorpe stared.

"Why am I?" he demanded. "What in God's name are you burbling about? The only articles I have purchased, praise be, are these gimcrack tables."

"I believe the attendants have already assembled most of your purchases," continued the auctioneer. "Would you like us to deliver, or will you arrange your own transport?"

"Transport?" Mr Bagthorpe shook his head uncomprehendingly.

"Oh – and here is your final account, if you will be so good as to settle it before removal. Rule of the house, I'm afraid, sir."

The auctioneer, still smiling, passed over a bill. Jack could see, even at a glance, that if it applied only to the tables, someone had gone into a very long description of them.

Mr Bagthorpe snatched the bill. He looked. He stared. A dark red flush stained his neck and face.

"A-shoo!" he sneezed. "A-shoo! One thousand three hundred and a-shoo – ninety-four pounds!"

He looked wildly about him, rendered temporarily speechless. His wife took the bill from his nerveless fingers.

"Oh dear!" she exclaimed. "It's true!"

Mr Bagthorpe sneezed again.

Eight

The Row that followed was, even by Bagthorpian standards, monumental. This was probably because Mr Bagthorpe realized, right from the word go, that he could not win. The small print (and possibly also the large) in the Conditions of Sale was against him.

He had ill-advisedly arranged that his secret bidding should be indicated by a stifled yawn. He had then had to sit still for nearly an hour while a procession of undesirable objects were brought forward and sold. At the best of times his boredom threshold was low. On this occasion his eyes became glazed very early on, through sheer lack of sleep. A man who has spent the greater part of the night roaming around the house stalking spooks is not likely to be at his most alert the following day.

Mr Bagthorpe had yawned fairly continuously throughout the proceedings. Some of these yawns had, by the law of averages, coincided with the final bids being made.

It would not have been so bad if he had acquired anything worthwhile—the odd Victorian chair, for instance, to supplement the deckchairs, or a few good oils that he could later have sold, possibly even at a profit.

The objects that Mr Bagthorpe's yawns had earned him were of truly spectacular awfulness and uselessness. They included two mounted stags' heads with massive, branching antlers, and a set of framed religious texts, such as 'Suffer Little Children to Come Unto Me'. There was a collection of antique umbrellas, none of them weatherproof, five rusting bicycles, a box full of military medals and ribbons, and a rocking-horse that looked as if it would never rock again. There were piles of what resembled dirty washing, but were apparently hand-stitched Victorian garments, and very valuable. (Nobody believed this, and Mrs Fosdyke later tore them up for cleaning rags.) Mr Bagthorpe had also yawned himself into a welter of bric à brac, the most repellent of which was probably a musical box lacquered in violent green and red that played, when opened, a rusty version of 'Home Sweet Home'.

Even Mrs Bagthorpe could find nothing Positive to say.

She cast vainly about, and was about to remark comfortingly that at least none of these items was too large, and so they could be transported at a low cost, when one of the attendants indicated a wardrobe at the rear of the room.

"We left that where it is," he told Mr Bagthorpe, "because we couldn't shift it – not just the three of us."

The wardrobe in question was the largest anyone present had ever seen. You could, as Mr Bagthorpe pointed out, have set up house in it, at a pinch.

"Knock out a couple of windows and install central heating, and you're there," he said. "You could even have two storeys, at a pinch."

He tried hard, at the time, to leave this majestic piece of furniture behind him, but was told this was out of the question.

"The house must be completely cleared," they said. "Everything must go."

In the end Mr Bagthorpe paid his bill and stamped off, leaving his wife to make arrangements about delivery. Jack, genuinely sorry for him, and fearing that he might do something rash, followed.

Mr Bagthorpe was already out of the drive and on the road, moving at a fast rate in the direction of Llosilli. Could he be intending to walk the thirty miles back, Jack wondered? If so, it would be a very uncharacteristic act. Mr Bagthorpe did not believe in exercise, which, he maintained, weakened the brain.

"It drains all the blood from the cells," he would explain. "It also, of course, leads to broken limbs and inflamed joints. I know many people who have died of it."

"That was really rotten luck, Father," said Jack, catching up with him.

"That," wheezed Mr Bagthorpe, who was already out of breath, "was not bad luck. It was a frame-up. A conspiracy. It was also bad judgement on my part in picking a wife. I admit it. Who else's wife would have bid against her own husband the way she did? Not even Lot's. Ha — lots. Pun. Get it?"

Jack was having trouble in keeping up with Mr Bagthorpe's stride.

"Where are we going?" he asked.

"Pub," came the brief reply. "Saw one, as we came."

Jack was relieved by this answer, which *was* in

character. He was himself very hungry. In fact, one of the reasons he had accompanied the auction party was the prospect of having a meal out. It was by now nearly two o'clock.

"What about the others?" he asked.

There was no reply other than a snort. Under the circumstances this was understandable. Jack could see that Mr Bagthorpe did not at the moment feel like treating the others to a meal.

The two of them had a hearty ploughman's lunch (washed down, in Mr Bagthorpe's case, with copious draughts of beer) and made their way back to the house. Their reception by the other three was frigid.

"*Really*, Henry!" said Mrs Bagthorpe. "It was too bad, going off like that without a word. We didn't know *what* had happened to you."

"If ever I commit suicide," returned her husband, "it will not be by jumping off a Welsh crag. Ha!"

"We just went down to the pub for some lunch," Jack explained. At this Mrs Bagthorpe became very tight-lipped and Grandma claimed that by now she was quite faint with hunger.

"I could eat a 'orse," Mrs Fosdyke told everybody.

The next hour was spent driving around looking for food. The pubs had by now closed, and while they saw a lot of sheep and rocks they saw not a single restaurant, café or even snack bar. In the end they stopped at a village shop, where Mrs Bagthorpe purchased a small pork pie each for herself and Mrs Fosdyke, some crisps, and fruit for Grandma. The atmosphere in the car was terrible. It was filled with the champing of crisps, the powerful smell of oranges, and barely contained feelings of dislike, if not outright hatred.

It was almost with relief that Jack saw Ty Cilion Duon ahead. This was short-lived. There, drawn up by the front door, was Uncle Parker's car.

"Oh my God!" exclaimed Mr Bagthorpe. "That is all I need to crown my day!"

Had he known it, the day was yet far from crowned.

"Bang into it, why don't you, Laura?" he went on. "Everyone else does. Why should we have the only undented car in Wales? Take a run at it."

As they entered, the house seemed uncannily quiet.

"William!" called Mrs Bagthorpe. "Tess!"

From the kitchen came a cheerful 'Halloo!' from Uncle Parker. The Bagthorpes found him and Aunt Celia reclining in deckchairs, set at the lowest notch. The maddening thing was that both of them, even in those hideous and primitive surrounds, looked supremely elegant and relaxed. They looked like an advertisement for cocktails.

"Hallo there, Henry," Uncle Parker greeted him. "Good pickings?"

"Has that infernal goat turned up?" returned Mr Bagthorpe.

"I believe there have been one or two sightings," replied Uncle Parker. "But probably false ones. You know the Welsh – full of rumour and superstition."

"That goat," said Mr Bagthorpe, "is more than a rumour – as they will discover to their cost. And of course, eventually to *yours*, Russell. Can you *afford* that daughter of yours? Where is she?"

"Tracking down dragons, I believe," replied Uncle Parker serenely.

"Darling Daisy is roaming the misty mountains,"

105

elaborated Aunt Celia dreamily. "She is under the spell of Wales, she is lost in myth."

"Have you seen Tess and William?" asked Mrs Bagthorpe, forestalling any comment her husband might have to make about this definition of Daisy and her recent activities.

"Gone up to our place, for a swim," Uncle Parker told her. "But you haven't answered my question, Henry. How was the sale?"

As if on cue there was the sound of heavy tyres on gravel. The furniture van had arrived with Mr Bagthorpe's purchases. The unloading of these under Uncle Parker's amused gaze was hideously embarrassing. As the parade of formica tables, mounted stags' heads and old bicycles was carried from the van and dumped in the hall, his eyebrows rose higher and higher. He did not know about Mr Bagthorpe's illjudged secret bidding, but guessed that his brother-in-law could not have acquired these horrible articles voluntarily.

"I am at a loss for words," he murmured.

He was not, of course.

As the five decrepit bicycles were unloaded, pieces fell from them left and right – pedals, handlebars, tyres.

"It is never worth buying such articles brand new," he remarked. "They depreciate so rapidly. I applaud your wisdom, Henry."

The grand finale, of course, was the wardrobe. To compound his humiliation, Mr Bagthorpe was obliged to give a hand with the unloading of this, though he refused to have it carried into the house, and it was merely placed to the side of the drive.

Uncle Parker had a field day.

"Great heavens!" he exclaimed. "A potting shed! What a very superior model – mahogany, and bevelled mirrors! But no – of course not! Too large. Could it – ?"

"Oh Russell, do stop!" pleaded Mrs Bagthorpe. On this occasion, Uncle Parker was rubbing rather too much salt into the wound.

Mr Bagthorpe, panting and perspiring freely, stared with repugnance for a few moments at the expensive pile of rubbish in the hall. He then, wordlessly, began to drag one of the formica tables towards his study. It made an excruciating screeching sound on the flagstones. He probably intended it to.

The door banged shut.

"Poor Henry," murmured Mrs Bagthorpe, who was too soft-hearted for her own good. "Perhaps he will be able to work off his feelings by creating."

"Let's get that other table in the kitchen, quick," suggested Mrs Fosdyke. "Else 'e'll 'ave it, as well. 'E's a real cow in the manger."

"Jack, dear," said Grandma, "would you please find an electrical point and plug in my new gramophone? I wish to play one of my operatic records. It will soothe my nerves."

Whether or not the racket that ensued had this effect was known only to Grandma herself. It certainly did nothing for anyone else's nerves. Quite the reverse. Jack, who did not know one opera from another, picked one entitled *The Valkyrie*, thinking it sounded fairly harmless.

The record was so badly cracked that the (worn) needle practically never lighted on a smooth patch. Nor was this all. One of the reasons why its previous owners had got rid of the gramophone must, presumably, have been because its engine was wearing out. It was not playing at 78 rpm, but at somewhere about the 70 mark. The distortion caused by this, plus the reverberations from the cracks and scratches, created what was virtually a new Art Form (the kind that receives large subsidies from the Arts Council).

Grandma, who had never listened to Wagner in her life, evidently thought this was how it was meant to sound.

"Heavenly," she murmured. "How consoling, and yet triumphant. Turn up the volume, Jack, please."

She wanted to make sure her son could hear it. Later, William had a go at the gramophone with a screwdriver, and managed to increase the rpm to around 75. Even then Grandma's repertoire of grand opera did not make for easy listening. The accoustics of the uncarpeted, uncurtained house did not help matters. It was, as Mr Bagthorpe later remarked, like having a whole pack of hyenas encamped up the chimney.

Jack noticed that Aunt Celia had both hands over her ears, and sympathized. You did not have to be hypersensitive, as she was, to be adversely affected by a racket of this order.

"I think we must take our leave," said Uncle Parker, obviously fearing for his wife's sanity.

"I think you should wait, and take Daisy with you," said Mrs Bagthorpe. "Did you not receive my note?"

"Note?"

"I left it with Rosie," she told him. "It was a request that she should return to the castle with you."

"Truth to tell, she's a mite bored up there, at present," Uncle Parker confessed. "Missing the goat. Happier down here, with you lot."

"I daresay," said Mrs Bagthorpe. "But what is in question, Russell, is not *her* happiness, but our own. We are already, as you can see, labouring under certain difficulties."

She was being unusually firm. The background music was probably bringing out her fighting spirit.

"Surely you would prefer to have Daisy with you, Celia?"

This appeal fell on deaf ears.

"I'll trot down later and fetch her," Uncle Parker promised. "Cheers, all! Lovely music!"

Jack, watching them speed off, thought how strange it was that Aunt Celia should not mind Daisy staying with his family so often.

"We're a bit accident-prone," he admitted to himself. "But there again, so's Daisy."

109

William and Tess now appeared, swimsuits under their arms.

"That was terrific," William said. "We had a snack by the pool, and charged it up to Uncle P."

"William!" exclaimed his mother reprovingly.

"Well, we're feeding Daisy," he argued. "Has she gone? Uncle P. whizzed past so fast I didn't see."

"She is still hunting for dragons with Rosie," his mother informed him.

"What's that awful row?" asked Tess. Then, seeing Mr Bagthorpe's bargains, "And what on earth's *this* lot?"

"She uses a lot shorter words these days," Jack thought. "Wales must be affecting her."

"Never mind that now," said Mrs Bagthorpe hastily, aware of her husband's brooding presence behind the nearby study door. "Go and see if there is anything you can do to help Mrs Fosdyke prepare the evening meal."

Jack felt lost without Zero, and wondered whether he was enjoying sniffing out dragons with Rosie and Daisy.

Zero was in fact the first member of the Dragon Hunt to reappear, though he was at first virtually unrecognizable. Daisy, presumably missing having Billy Goat Gruff to adorn, had set to with a will on Zero. She had attached to him a plethora of bows, streamers and bells. These he had clearly made every effort to shake off, thus enmeshing himself even further. He was so swathed in bands of pink satin as to resemble a high-class mummy. He also emitted a high tinkling.

William and Tess fell into fits of unfeeling laughter

110

at his entrance and the latter fetched her camera, in the absence of Rosie as official photographer.

Jack, on the other hand, was appalled. He alone knew how sensitive Zero was, and how easily undermined. He pulled desperately at the satin bands, but in the end had to fetch scissors to cut him free. It seemed to him that Zero's eyes were rolling in his head.

"It could've unhinged him," he thought. "It could mark him for life. I'll kill that Daisy."

So powerful a force was that child, even in her absence, that nobody would have been overly surprised had she eventually marched in towing a genuine Welsh dragon, fire and all, behind her. William said as much.

"And even *that*'ll be looped in ribbons," he said "–if she's got any left."

In the event, the hunting party arrived back at Ty Cilion Duon seriously depleted. It was a party of one–namely, Rosie.

She came running in at the front door and tripped straight over the new pile of junk.

"Quick, everybody, quick!" she screamed, scrambling to her feet. "Daisy's lost! Daisy's lost!"

The door of the study whipped open.

"Hallelujah!" yelled Mr Bagthorpe above the

111

competing Wagner. "Praise be! Amen!"

The door slammed shut. Mrs Bagthorpe came hurrying from the kitchen.

"Rosie!" she exclaimed. "What was that? I can't hear."

Nobody could hear. The Bagthorpes were no strangers to raised voices, but from now on would have to yell more or less as a matter of course.

"Daisy, poor little Daisy!" Rosie cried. "She's gone, she's vanished! What if a dragon's got her?"

"Amen!" came a triumphant shout from behind the study door. Mr Bagthorpe evidently had his ear to it.

"Calm down, Rosie, do," commanded Mrs Bagthorpe. It was a pity she could not give the same instructions to Brünnhilde, who was now waxing hysterical on Grandma's next record. "Tell us exactly what has happened."

"I don't know!" wailed Rosie. "All I know is, she's not here!"

"Then God's in his heaven," remarked Tess, "and all's right with the world."

"I'll kill her when she does turn up," added Jack. Normally he would have been sympathetic to Daisy's plight, lost and alone on a Welsh mountain. That was before Zero had been belled and ribboned.

"Come and *look* for her!" cried Rosie. "Everybody – quick!"

Grandma now appeared and was given the news.

"Telephone the police, Laura," she instructed. "At once!"

"There is no telephone!" said Mrs Bagthorpe helplessly.

112

"I think we ought to leave the police out of it," William said. "She'll turn up. She always does."

"More's the pity!" added the voice from the study.

"It's true," agreed Mrs Bagthorpe. "She does . . . and it *is* daylight . . ."

"Most murders," said Grandma, "contrary to popular belief, do not take place during the hours of darkness, but in broad daylight. It is sometimes difficult to believe, Laura, that you are an appointed Magistrate, and sit on the Bench."

"We must let Russell know," said poor Mrs Bagthorpe. "I will telephone him at once. Oh – I can't!"

She was rapidly going into a downward spiral. She was going the same way as Brünnhilde.

"I'll go and tell him!" volunteered William like a flash.

"You've already had your nosh for the day," Jack told him. "Me'n Zero'll go."

A minor squabble then set up and threatened to divert interest from the main issue altogether. Rosie, seeing this, started to scream, "Go and look for her, go and look! She might be being eaten alive!"

"Oh, surely not!" cried Mrs Bagthorpe, though without real conviction. "Oh, quickly, everyone, do go and look!"

One by one and grudgingly they were nearly all pressed into service. Mr Bagthorpe, needless to say, declined to join them. Grandma said that she, too, would remain behind. Someone had to be at the centre of the operation, she said, and besides, she was in need of the soothing influence of music. Mrs Fosdyke turned down the invitation to join the search point blank.

113

"*I* ain't going stumping over bogs looking for '*er*," she said.

Slowly the house emptied. The Bagthorpes scattered on the all too familiar mission of hunting Daisy. Ty Cilion Duon was left to the three remaining members of the household and its own Black Corners and, of course, Brünnhilde.

Nine

So taken up were they with Daisy's disappearance, the Bagthorpes failed to notice that another of their number was missing. This would be the second time in as many days that they had mislaid Grandpa. It seemed in danger of becoming a habit. It was not, however, until later that his absence was registered.

The way the Bagthorpes set about looking for Daisy was very desultory and half-hearted. They were all, basically, sick of looking for Daisy. Moreover, they did not care if they never found her. Mrs Bagthorpe was the most conscientious of the search party, and scampered hither and thither in a state of mounting lather. She tried valiantly to Think Positively, but found this difficult, on account of the visions she kept having of Daisy sucked up to her neck in a Welsh bog.

Jack took the opportunity of putting Zero through his paces as a tracker. He pushed a fistful of the cut-up satin garlands under Zero's nose.

"Now – find!" he commanded. "Atta, boy – seek out! Find Daisy!"

Zero certainly set off at a fair lick, but this was no guarantee that he had picked up a scent, or even that he had understood his instructions. Jack followed, thinking that if Zero did track down Daisy, it would be entirely to his credit, and show what a lovely nature he had. Plenty of dogs, having been tied up in knots with satin and bells, would have let her rot (or even bitten her).

Tess wandered about the grounds of Ty Cilion Duon calling Daisy's name occasionally, and then, when well clear of the house, took out a paperback about the secret power of pyramids and went behind a bush to read it. A hundred yards away, had she known it, William was similarly engaged – except that his book was about electronics. Every now and then he looked up from it to reflect on the general hatefulness of Wales, and wonder whether he would ever speak to Anonymous from Grimsby again.

After about an hour members of the alleged search party arrived back at the house one by one to report having drawn a blank. The general angst was not helped by the deafening strains of 'The Ride of the Valkyries', which Grandma thought the most effective record she had tried so far, and had already played five times.

"I dread to think what the tabloids will make of the story, Laura," she told her daughter-in-law. "They will make much, no doubt, of your being a Magistrate, and you can probably say goodbye to your column forever. When Daisy's loss is reported, the name of Stella Bright will be anathema to the British Public."

"Oh, do not say such things!" cried Mrs Bagthorpe, and shot off in the car to inform Uncle Parker of Daisy's latest disappearance.

116

Jack himself was surprised that Grandma should sound so cool. If she really *did* think Daisy was dead, she was taking the loss of her favourite remarkably calmly. He wandered round to the back of the house, where Mrs Fosdyke seemed to have got quite a creditable stew going on the camping stove. She had probably been spurred on by her own lack of a proper lunch. He was surprised to see Rosie squatting nearby, scraping carrots.

"Why aren't you still looking for Daisy?" he demanded.

"Poor little Daisy," said Rosie sadly.

Jack stared.

"Is that all you can say?"

She gave a little sniff then, and rubbed her sleeve over her eyes, though Jack could see no sign of tears.

"Poor little Daisy," she said again.

Mrs Fosdyke appeared, and gave her stew a brisk stir.

"I always knew that that Daisy'd come to a bad end," she said with satisfaction. "It'll be a wonder if they ever find her corpse."

Mrs Bagthorpe returned to announce that Uncle Parker had himself set out in search of Daisy.

"He does not think we should involve the police at this stage," she said, "and he has not told Celia. She thinks that Daisy is still with us."

Jack was, by and large, disgusted with the lot of them.

"You'd think," he told Zero, "that they'd lost a paper clip, not a living human being." (He, unlike his father, was prepared to accord Daisy the status of a member of the human race.)

117

"Even Grandma," he went on. "Even Rosie. They just don't seem to care. I know Daisy's always turned up before, but it doesn't mean to say she necessarily will this time. There's a first time for everything. And a last," he added, as an afterthought. He almost felt like crying.

Mr Bagthorpe was at least consistent in his reactions. He had never pretended to like Daisy, nor, now, did he pretend he cared whether or not she would ever be seen again. Indeed, he said, he relished the prospect of Life Without Daisy.

"It will be one fewer thorn in my flesh," he said, "though God knows it still leaves plenty."

"After supper, you and me'll go and look for her again, old chap," Jack told Zero. He had it at the back of his mind that if Daisy *were* lost for ever, so, too, would Aunt Celia be before long. He thought it likely that she would become unhinged and do away with herself. She would, naturally, go about this in a very poetic way. She would probably strew flowers around, and put them in her hair, and then go floating (face upwards, of course) down a Welsh river, like Ophelia.

The Family, drawn by the delicious scent of Mrs Fosdyke's stew, assembled for supper. Even Mr Bagthorpe assembled.

"Is this a Welsh Stew, Mrs Fosdyke?" asked Mrs Bagthorpe brightly. "How clever of you!"

"It ain't Welsh," replied Mrs Fosdyke. "It's one of them French ones."

"Jack, dear, go and find your grandfather," said his mother, "and tell him supper is ready."

Now Grandpa's disappearance was discovered. So

little did he impinge on their lives that no one could even remember when they had last seen him. The only thing they could be absolutely certain of was that he had been there at breakfast-time.

"When did *you* last see him?" Mr Bagthorpe asked Grandma. "He is, after all, your husband."

"That does not make him my responsibility," she replied. "He is eighty-five, and old enough to take care of himself. He has probably gone fishing again, and fallen into a river."

Members of the family were now being written off at an alarming rate, it seemed to Jack.

"That makes *three*," he thought, "counting Aunt Celia."

It would also, of course, mean that if the Welsh police were informed, they would have three searches on their hands – counting the goat. Jack was reminded of Mrs Fosdyke's often repeated assertion that "things always go in threes". It began to look as though there might be some truth in this.

"I had better drive down to the village and make inquiries," said Mrs Bagthorpe.

"I was thinking I might 'ave an hour in The 'Arp myself," remarked Mrs Fosdyke. "See if Mavis or Megan is there."

If so, she reflected, there would be plenty more to tell them. On the other hand, there was no guarantee that they would be in there, and she did not know where they lived. Despite the warmth and closeness of the friendships that had developed during the previous evening, she had quite neglected to learn their addresses.

"Oooh yes, go on, do!" cried Rosie.

This foxed Jack. Rosie was no more interested in Mrs Fosdyke and her doings than anyone else, so far as he knew.

"I'll do the washing up," Rosie offered. "I'll do all of it, by myself."

This was so out of character as to indicate that she had gone clean out of her mind.

"I'll just fetch my 'at and coat," Mrs Fosdyke told her employer.

She had, of course, plenty of minor acquaintances in The Welsh Harp. There was no real danger of her sitting nursing her Guinness alone in a corner.

The pair of them accordingly set off in the car. Tess announced her intention of going up to the castle for another bath, and William too disappeared, probably afraid that Rosie would change her mind about the washing up. Mr Bagthorpe retreated to his study, and Grandma went and rummaged among her records for suitable background music—or rather, in this case, foreground.

"Come on," Jack told Zero. "We'll go and look for Daisy."

He pushed the satin ribbons under Zero's nose again, and they set off.

"It won't be your fault if you don't track her down," Jack told Zero. "Her scent's probably gone cold."

On the other hand, he thought, Daisy probably had a very powerful scent. She was certainly a very powerful personality and, moreover, seldom took a bath.

Jack very much wanted to find Daisy. He thought her, despite her many shortcomings, likeable and warm-hearted. He had even found himself in sympathy when Uncle Parker had confessed to her pathological fear of going down the plughole. This had reminded him that when he himself was small, he had been frightened of being sucked down the lavatory. He would pull the chain and run like mad. He had not, naturally, admitted to this phobia.

He had just reached the edge of the grounds, where only a broken fence marked the wilderness of Ty Cilion Duon from the general wilderness of Wales, when an idea struck him. He remembered noticing, among the jumbled heaps of Mr Bagthorpe's auction bargains, a large brass handbell.

"I bet that's got a really loud clang," he thought. "I bet it'd carry a lot further than me shouting. It might even reach Daisy *and* Grandpa."

He found the idea of killing two birds with one stone, thus making himself the hero of the hour, attractive. He accordingly turned back again to the house.

As he approached he heard first the fractured tones of the Vienna State Opera Company and then, above it, the screaming of Rosie. She sounded quite hysterical.

"She's gone! She's gone!"

This seemed to be what she was screaming. To whom, he wondered, could this apply? He rapidly worked out that, as the other female members of the household had departed on stated missions, it must be Grandma. This was certainly the logical conclusion. On the other hand, Grandma was not the kind of person who *did* go missing. She was virtually unlosable.

As he entered the hall Grandma was just emerging from the chairless sitting-room, where she had been performing her role as resident disc jockey. Rosie was still having hysterics in the kitchen. Jack charged in and Rosie lifted her tear-stained face hopefully. She saw him, and it immediately crumpled again.

"What's up, Rosie?" Jack asked.

"Oh, she's gone! Darling little Daisy, she's not there!"

"Not where?" probed Jack.

"In her nest!"

This reply gave Jack pause. It appeared that Rosie was temporarily deranged by grief.

"Look, Rosie," he said kindly, "cheer up. She'll turn up. And—and Daisy hasn't *got* a nest."

"She has, she has!" cried Rosie passionately. She pointed dramatically.

She seemed, improbably, to be pointing at the boiler. Jack, thinking to humour her, went round it. The door was wide open. Inside there seemed to be a little heap of clothes. It looked rather as if someone had mistaken the boiler for a washing machine.

"You see!" cried Rosie. "She's not there!"

It had not even occurred to Jack that she might be.

"I don't get it," he said. "Why on earth should she be?"

"Because we'd made her a *nest*!" Rosie cried. "We got all woolly jumpers and soft things and made it really cosy."

At this point Mrs Bagthorpe returned, having dropped off Mrs Fosdyke at The Welsh Harp.

"Has your grandfather returned?" she inquired anxiously.

"No, he hasn't," Jack told her. "And now Daisy's disappeared."

"But—but Daisy is already lost," she said bewilderedly.

Jack shook his head.

"She was meant to be in her nest."

The whole story then came out. Apparently Rosie had read the message left by Mrs Bagthorpe for Uncle Parker, requesting Daisy's immediate return to the castle. This had not suited her book at all. The pair of them had then decided that Daisy's best course would be to hide. Unfortunately Ty Cilion Duon, because of the sparseness of its furnishings, did not offer many suitable hiding-places. But William had cleaned out the boiler, and the idea of Daisy's setting up house in there had appealed strongly to them. The idea was certainly original, Jack thought, even by Daisy's own exacting standards.

Mr Bagthorpe, when he was apprised of the situation, thought the same.

"You would search the annals of the world in vain," he said, "for evidence of anyone ever having

123

gone to live in a boiler. Even Diogenes would have drawn the line there. Are you sure she's not in there, up one of those rusty spouts?"

The plan had been that Rosie should come running in with the news that Daisy had disappeared. Then, when the whole household had scattered in search of her, Daisy was to nip in through the back door and establish herself in the boiler.

"But I bet Fozzy never went to look for her!" cried Rosie. "I bet she was there all the time in the kitchen."

"I do believe she was," agreed Mrs Bagthorpe.

"Well, I thought Daisy was in the boiler," Rosie said tearfully. "And when Fozzy had gone, I was going to give her some food. I'd got a little feast for her."

"So *that*'s why you said you'd do the washing up!" exclaimed Jack, light dawning.

"I must say I think it a remarkably silly plan," observed Grandma. "I do not consider a boiler a natural habitat for darling Daisy."

"If we'd then lit the fire, it would've been," said Mr Bagthorpe. "Ha!"

"You be quiet, you be quiet!" Rosie screamed.

In the hall the Vienna State Opera Company acted as Greek Chorus.

"Look!" shouted Mr Bagthorpe, coming in as solo baritone, "I cannot stand much more of this *din*!"

He strode out of the kitchen, there was the sound of clattering and cursing as he tripped over his bric à brac, and then – peace.

"Oh – what has he done?" cried Grandma in tones of epic despair.

She rushed to investigate and Jack followed. His father was in the sitting-room, holding the plug of the gramophone. He was trying to wrench the flex out of it. But at least he had not gone for the actual machine and pile of records with a sledgehammer, as he had already threatened to do several times. And Jack was forced to admit that all of a sudden it did seem to be very peaceful, even with Rosie still caterwauling. His sympathies definitely lay with his father.

Mr Bagthorpe had a very low threshold of tolerance to noise (though was presumably immune to any made by himself, which was plenty). He took all noises personally. Even a harmless bluebottle, buzzing in his study on a summer's day, would be accused of deliberately sabotaging his creativity, and would be relentlessly pursued with an aerosol can, and exterminated. Jack had once come across him in the garden hurling abuse at the pilot of a low-flying aircraft. He had then thrown his spade at it.

"Ha!" The flex and the plug parted, and Mr Bagthorpe waved the latter triumphantly.

"That's put paid to *that* bunch of hyenas!" he yelled.

"It is a pity, Henry," said Grandma coldly, "that you are so totally devoid of culture. And what a very childish act. Give me the plug immediately, please. William shall fix it on again for me."

Mr Bagthorpe whipped the plug behind his back.

"I most certainly will not!" he said.

Jack watched the pair of them with interest. This was certainly a very direct confrontation, a real power struggle. Surely Grandma would not try to wrest the plug from Mr Bagthorpe's grasp? And if she did, would he release it? Surely even he would not engage in a wrestling match with his own mother?

This Jack would never know. There came a spurting of gravel, rapid footsteps, and Uncle Parker burst into the hall. Jack had never seen him move so fast. It was not his style. (He did jog, but that was in private.)

"Any sign?" he gasped. He did not go in for gasping, either, as a rule. He had been severely tested by his offspring right from birth, he had been subjected to Fire, Flood and Arry Awk, to name but three of his trials. He had remained relaxed, even amused. Now, however, it would seem that he had finally lost his cool.

"Ah, Russell, dear," Grandma greeted him. "You have arrived most fortunately. I have a small electrical repair I wish you would make for me."

"Over my dead body," gritted Mr Bagthorpe. "Are you aware, Russell, that your daughter is now nesting in boilers?"

Uncle Parker appeared genuinely dazed. He looked speechlessly from one to the other. He was quite pale.

"Ah, Russell!" exclaimed Mrs Bagthorpe, emerging from the kitchen, where she had been trying vainly to comfort Rosie. "Thank heavens you have come! Daisy is missing again."

"Again?" echoed Uncle Parker bewilderedly. "What—you mean you've found her, then lost her again?"

"Ah—well, not exactly," she said. "It is all rather difficult to explain. You had better come and look at this."

126

Uncle Parker followed her meekly into the kitchen, where he was shown Daisy's empty nest in the boiler.

Jack looked again at the forlorn little heap of clothes and found himself strangely moved by it. It seemed to him very innocent and touching that Daisy should have thought of setting up her secret home in there. It was also, of course, a compliment to the Bagthorpes.

"She likes us," he thought, "even if most of us don't like her. She wanted to stay here with us."

"Well, Russell, what have you to say to *that*?" demanded Mr Bagthorpe.

Uncle Parker was staring at the boiler, shaking his head.

"I don't understand," he admitted at length.

It was all beyond him. The way Daisy's mind worked was beyond anybody, if it came to that.

"Father is missing, too," Mrs Bagthorpe told him. "It is now nearly dark. It is time to telephone the police."

"How many more times, Laura," said her husband wearily, "do we have to remind you that there *is* no telephone. No telephone, no hot water, no television, no—"

"Oh, be *quiet*!" snapped his wife, and immediately clapped a hand to her mouth. She then took several very deep breaths. The calming power of yoga had never been more needed than here, recently, in Wales.

Jack noticed that Zero had padded over to the front door and gone out. He followed.

"I don't want him to disappear," he thought. "I'd kill myself."

The lights of Uncle Parker's car shone on the vast

127

mahogany and mirrored wardrobe that stood like a megalith on the verge. Zero was standing by it. His head was cocked to one side, as if he were listening. He was sniffing and snuffling, too.

"Zero!" Jack called. Zero turned his head for a moment, but did not come. The way the light was tipping his fur, it seemed possible that it was standing up on end.

"Surely there can't be Black Corners in *there*?" Jack thought. "It doesn't even belong to this house."

On the other hand, it had come from another very old house. For all Jack knew, Wales was awash with old houses with Black Corners.

He did not much feel like investigating.

"After all, it might not be a ghost," he thought. "It might be a murderer. It would be really silly for me to tackle a murderer on my own."

He poked his head back round the door. He could hear raised voices, and Rosie still sobbing.

"I think you ought to come and look!" he called. "I think Zero's found something out here."

"The day that mutton-headed hound finds anything," said Mr Bagthorpe, more or less automatically, "will be the day pigs fly – backwards."

He remained in the kitchen with the distraught Rosie. Uncle Parker and Mrs Bagthorpe, however, obeyed the summons, followed by Grandma.

"I'll go and have a look," said Uncle Parker, when Zero's strange behaviour was pointed out to him. "He may, of course, just be sizing it up prior to cocking a leg."

He went over to the wardrobe and stood for a moment with his ear to it. Then, without warning, he whipped open the door.

He stood staring into its cavernous interior as if transfixed. Zero, on the other hand, relaxed, and began wagging his tail.

"Come on," Jack told his mother.

They, too, went over and peered inside. There, curled up on what looked like a sleeping wolf, thumb in mouth and fast asleep, was Daisy Parker.

Ten

So peaceful, so utterly contented did Daisy look, that Jack found it hard to believe that it was really she. He had never, he realized, seen Daisy asleep before. Few people had. She kept very irregular hours for a five-year-old. Whatever time she had gone to bed she was always up and doing at the crack of dawn.

"Bless her little heart!" breathed Mrs Bagthorpe ecstatically, and, Jack felt, rather wetly. "Doesn't she look sweet?"

"Do close the door," came Grandma's voice behind them. "She is in a draught, and will catch cold."

Jack, peering more closely into the wardrobe, saw that the sleeping wolf was in fact Grandma's fur coat. The plot appeared to be thickening. Jack recalled Grandma's earlier calm reaction to the news that Daisy was missing.

"You would think to look at her," said Uncle Parker in awed tones, "that she would not harm a fly."

Even with her thumb in her mouth Daisy seemed to be smiling. She was probably dreaming of Fire and Flood, of Arry Awk and funerals, and wrecked police cars.

130

Tess now reappeared, fresh from her sunken bath at the castle.

"I've had a lovely time," she announced. "I've been teaching Aunt Celia White Magic, and she's going to take it up. What are you all doing out here?"

Jack indicated the wardrobe.

"Good grief!" she exclaimed. "What's she doing in there? Is she going to live there, or what?"

Mr Bagthorpe, fed up with Rosie's non-stop sobbing, and not wishing to miss anything, now appeared. He overheard this last remark, and seized the opportunity to attempt a quick resale of the wardrobe.

"*That*'s an idea!" he said. "How about it, Russell? It's plenty big enough to accommodate her hellish goat as well, if and when it turns up."

"I do not think Celia will see Daisy as the inmate of a wardrobe," Uncle Parker replied, his cool returning by the moment now that Daisy was found.

"It would certainly strain her symbolism," agreed Mr Bagthorpe, "but would strike her as preferable to a boiler, I should think."

He craned forward past the others.

"What's that animal she's got in there with her?" he demanded. "Is it the goat?"

"No, Henry, it is not," Grandma told him. "It is my fur coat. It has never been put to better use."

"You mean to say," said Mr Bagthorpe, "that you *knew* she was holed up in here, all along? That you aided and abetted her?"

"Certainly I did," she replied calmly, "though I do not care for your terminology. The words 'aid

131

and abet' would seem to suggest a crime. You should learn to use words accurately, Henry. Reposing in wardrobes is not a crime."

An argument was here forestalled by the return of William. He had gone out partly to avoid helping with either the washing up or the hunt for his missing relatives, and partly to see if he could find a tennis court anywhere.

"If I have to miss the whole season through being trapped in Wales without a single practice," he had told his father earlier, "I shall charge you up with the £100,000 odd I would've eventually got for winning Wimbledon."

He, too, was now shown Daisy, and was predictably disgusted.

"Just like a skunk in a hole!" he said. "Is that another skunk, in there with her?"

"No, William, it is not," Grandma told him. "It is my fur coat. I shall leave it to Daisy in my will." She paused. "Along with the rest of my Estate."

To her disappointment, nobody took this up. As far as the rest of the Bagthorpes were concerned, Grandma appeared indestructible. Nobody wasted time thinking about her possible demise.

"But why, Mother, did you *put* Daisy in the wardrobe?" asked Mrs Bagthorpe. "And why did you not tell us that she was here? We have been beside ourselves with anxiety for her welfare."

"*I* haven't," said Mr Bagthorpe.

"Because, Laura," replied Grandma, ignoring her son, "you were heartlessly casting her off. The child asks nothing more than to be allowed to stay with us and search for dragons and ghosties – ghosts. Even

Rosie saw the injustice and inhumanity of that note you left for Russell."

"But why is she in the wardrobe rather than the boiler?" persisted Mrs Bagthorpe, making a mental note to put any further communications into a sealed envelope.

"Because Mrs Fosdyke was in the kitchen," replied Grandma, "and she, perverse creature that she is, has no fondness for darling Daisy. I therefore used my initiative and offered her an alternative hiding-place. I have an exceptionally clear head in a crisis."

"Which is just as well," put in her son, "given the number of them you yourself precipitate."

"But she might have suffocated," protested Mrs Bagthorpe.

"I am not a fool, Laura," Grandma told her. "I took an axe from the hall, and made an air vent."

So she had. On one side of the wardrobe a long jagged crack could be discerned, even in that light.

"Hell fire!" exclaimed Mr Bagthorpe. "That does it! Either you, Mother, must reimburse me for the full cost, or you, Russell, must buy it. Your daughter has, in any case, established squatter's rights."

"I shall not pay you a penny," Grandma told him. "The crack I have made improves the item. It now looks genuinely antique. Before, it might very well have been taken for a reproduction."

"Right, Russell, it's yours. I'll fetch the bill, and you can settle for it now."

He lurched off.

"Henry is utterly obsessed by money," Grandma remarked. "It is one of the ways you can tell he is not a true writer—one of the *many* ways."

At this point the scene suddenly brightened, lit by another pair of headlights and the all too familiar steady flashing of a blue light.

"The police!" cried Grandma, enchanted. This was all that was needed to complete her happiness. She went to greet them.

"Good evening, officers. All is well, I trust?"

Mrs Bagthorpe too hurried forward, hoping to enlist them in the search for Grandpa, by now forgotten again by most persons but herself.

"Good evening, Ma'am," returned Policeman One. "We were informed that a Mr Parker might be here."

"Russell!" shouted Mr Bagthorpe, emerging from the house. "You're wanted. It's the fuzz!"

"Keep your voice down, please," said Grandma. "You will wake Daisy."

"We've just come down from the castle, sir," Policeman Two told Uncle Parker. "You're wanted up there directly. Your wife is in a state of shock."

"Hysterics," put in One.

"Think nothing of it," Mr Bagthorpe told them. "She is rarely otherwise. You certainly picked unlucky when you picked Celia, Russell. If she—"

He broke off. There was a roar, a shower of stones, and Uncle Parker was gone, missing the police car by inches.

"See that?" yelled Mr Bagthorpe, thwarted of his prey. "Sixty miles an hour, in a drive! Get after him! Book him!"

He might not have spoken for all the notice the policemen took. They had already agreed, on the drive down from the castle, to conduct their business with all possible speed, and retreat. They had no intention of bandying words with the Bagthorpes, who had already become a byword amongst the Welsh force for bringing ill luck. It was widely believed that no one who tangled with the Bagthorpes would get promoted, ever.

"Sorry to have troubled you, sir," said One, and they both walked firmly back to their car. "Goodnight!"

The car made a neat turn, and the Bagthorpes watched its receding taillights disappear round the first bend in the drive.

"My God!" exclaimed Mr Bagthorpe in disgust. "They could have had him there! They – "

"I wonder what can be the matter with poor Celia?" interrupted Mrs Bagthorpe in worried tones. "Perhaps she is distraught over Daisy's disappearance, though the police did not *mention* Daisy . . ."

"I expect that goat's killed someone," Mr Bagthorpe told her. "I said it would, I've said so all along. And Daisy, as its owner, will take the rap."

"You realize, don't you," said William, "that we've still *got* Daisy?"

All eyes swung back to the wardrobe.

"You'd better yank her out, Mother," he continued, "and take her back up there. Uncle Park won't be back tonight."

"But . . . but if poor Celia is in such a state . . ." faltered Mrs Bagthorpe.

"Daisy must not be disturbed," Grandma said. "She is in a deep, peaceful slumber. I shall fetch a rug to cover her with, and we will all take turns to guard her through the night."

What she meant was that everyone else would.

"You're joking," said Tess.

"Hang on a minute," said Mr Bagthorpe, "that is good thinking, Mother. If she spends the night in the wardrobe, it will clinch the sale to Russell. It will constitute a possession. Possession is nine points of the law."

"I was not thinking of your sale, Henry," Grandma told him, annoyed that she had unwittingly played into his hands. "I was thinking of Daisy, who has an exceptionally highly tuned nervous system, in common with most geniuses."

"'Alloo!" came a call in familiar tones.

The Bagthorpes turned to see approaching the figures of Mrs Fosdyke and Grandpa, arm in arm.

"Father!" cried Mrs Bagthorpe with tremendous relief. "Oh, what a lucky day this has been!" she added Positively.

"Lucky?" echoed her husband. "Lucky? Today has been an unmitigated disaster from start to finish. It has been little short of Armageddon. I sometimes think, Laura –"

"Oooh, we've 'ad ever such a lovely time, Mr Bagthorpe Senior and me!" announced Mrs Fosdyke

happily, interrupting her employer's flow. "I found 'im in The 'Arp, you know. 'E wasn't lost at all!"

The pair of them stood there, arms still hooked, beaming. Most present found this extremely irritating.

"You have been most thoughtless, Alfred," Grandma told her spouse.

He continued to beam, thus seeming to indicate that he was being S.D. (Selectively Deaf—hearing only what he wished to hear.)

"We 'ad a lovely game of dominoes, didn't we?" continued Mrs Fosdyke.

"We did indeed. And very well you played, too," replied her escort gallantly.

Mrs Fosdyke smirked. Mr Bagthorpe's fingers itched.

"Was you out looking for us?" inquired Mrs Fosdyke. Seeing the entire family standing outside in the darkness must have prompted this optimistic inquiry. Not one of them would even have crossed the road to look for Mrs Fosdyke.

"I rather think I prefer playing dominoes to watching the television," said Grandpa.

No one took much interest in this observation. Most of Grandpa's existence was spent following harmless pursuits well out of his family's way. The playing of dominoes did not present much of a departure from this norm. All they asked was that next time he went off he should tell them, thus saving them the bother of looking for him.

"Oooh, we've 'ad ever such laughs!" Mrs Fosdyke told everyone, seriously misjudging their interest in her evening. "You should've 'eard 'em all 'oot and roar when I told 'em about Mr Bagthorpe doing all that

137

yawning at that sale! Thought it was the funniest thing they'd ever 'eard!"

Mr Bagthorpe fixed her with a murderous glare.

"There is," he gritted, "such a thing as the law of slander."

"Ah, but that don't apply," returned Mrs Fosdyke smugly. "It only applies when things ain't true. Was true, this was."

She considered herself something of an authority on the laws of libel and slander. Mr Bagthorpe was so often threatening to invoke them that she had got her solicitor to explain them to her when visiting him to make her will. (She had made her will quite soon after entering the Bagthorpes' employ.)

"What did them police want?" she continued. "Went past us, they did, ever so fast. 'Ave they dredged up that Daisy's corpse?"

"She's in there," Jack told her, and pointed to the wardrobe.

Mrs Fosdyke's eyes stretched wide. She advanced cautiously.

"Dead?" she asked in a hoarse whisper.

"Sleeping," Grandma corrected, "and in a serious draught. She would by now be safely tucked up in the boiler, if it were not for yourself, Mrs Fosdyke."

"Tucked up?" echoed Mrs Fosdyke. "Boiler?"

She was shaking her head. After an evening of comparative normality in The Welsh Harp, she was now back in the land of Oz. Shades of the Bagthorpe household were already closing about her.

"Fetch a rug, Jack, please," Grandma told him, "and then you shall be First Watch. The others can cast lots for their turns."

At this Tess and William flatly stated that they did not intend to guard Daisy at any stage during her night in the wardrobe. They did not care a fig, they said, *what* happened to her—indeed, they rather hoped something would.

"Her own goat might even polish her off," William said. "*That*'d be poetic justice—even Aunt Celia would have to agree on that."

"*You* do it, Father," Tess told him. "It's your wardrobe. With any luck, it might even be haunted."

Most of the others tittered.

"If that brat is woken now," Mr Bagthorpe told them, "she will be thoroughly refreshed. She's had five hours' kip already, and that's par for the course for her. She will then roam about the house all night destroying things right and left, and *no one* will get any sleep."

A little silence followed this speech. His audience knew it to be the truth. The alternatives facing them were bleak.

"What a dilemma," murmured Mrs Bagthorpe. "But I do think you are right, Henry. To leave her sleeping here will be the lesser of two evils."

"I'm off to bed," announced Mrs Fosdyke in disgust.

She stumped off. Grandpa beamed round at everybody, said goodnight, and followed her.

"Much as I adore that sweet child," said Grandma, "I fear that I am precluded from taking a Watch myself because of my age, and frail constitution."

"Bilge, Mother," Mr Bagthorpe told her. "You're as tough as an ox."

Grandma was already on her way. She turned.

139

"Goodnight, everyone," she said. "I will remember you all in my prayers."

"You leave me out of them!" yelled Mr Bagthorpe after her.

"Zero could guard," Jack suggested.

There was another silence. As a rule, all the Bagthorpes would have poured scorn on this suggestion, and thrown in a few insults for good measure. None of them believed that Zero could guard, but on the other hand they did not care whether he could or not, on this occasion. They were not remotely concerned whether or not Daisy was kidnapped in the night. Moreover, this solution would neatly let them all off the hook.

"Good thinking, Jack," said William warmly.

Mr Bagthorpe opened his mouth to make one of his customary dismissive remarks about Zero, then closed it again. He, too, could see the advantages of the scheme, and he was probably more in need of a night's sleep than anyone else. He had tried to catnap in his study earlier, but had been prevented by Tristan and Isolde.

"Oh, I really don't know . . ." said Mrs Bagthorpe.

"I'll stay with him, Mother," Jack told her, "in my sleeping bag. I really like sleeping outside."

"Good old Jack," said Tess. "Don't fuss, Mother. You don't have to be a genius to guard a wardrobe."

She, too, made for the house. She turned.

"And if he wants a relief," she said, "let Rosie do it. The whole thing's her fault."

"Hang on," said William. "Where *is* Rosie?"

No one knew.

"She *was* in the kitchen," Jack said. "Bawling."

But that had been some time ago. And as so often was the case with the Bagthorpes, a lot of water had gone under the bridge since then. Rosie had not witnessed the discovery of Daisy in the wardrobe, the visits from Uncle Parker and the police, nor the reappearance of Grandpa.

"Oh dear, I must go and look!" cried Mrs Bagthorpe. She made for the house at a fast rate, followed by the rest. Jack gently closed the wardrobe door and went after them, to fetch his sleeping bag.

"You and me've got a really important job to do tonight, old chap," he told Zero.

When the Bagthorpes entered the kitchen its only occupant was Mrs Fosdyke, who was making herself a nightcap of milky cocoa.

"Oh—have you seen Rosie?" asked Mrs Bagthorpe.

"No, I ain't," replied Mrs Fosdyke unhelpfully. "And I ain't looking for 'er, neither. The rate folks go missing in this 'ouse is a disgrace."

Ungracious as this comment was, Jack could not help feeling that there was some truth in it. The Bagthorpes really were going missing at an unprecedented rate.

Mrs Fosdyke poured the milk into her mug, stirred it noisily, turned, and half-tripped over Zero, thereby splashing cocoa all over the place, including her second best outfit.

"Drat and 'ell!" she screeched. "What's 'e *doing*, everlasting under my feet!"

What Zero appeared to be doing, having recovered from the initial shock of being tripped over, was sniffing at the boiler and wagging his tail. Jack went

141

round to him. There, lying in Daisy's intended nest, was Rosie, fast asleep.

"It's Rosie!" he exclaimed. "She's gone to sleep in there!"

"Oh my God!" said Mr Bagthorpe. "It must be infectious. We'll *all* end up in the boiler!"

Mrs Fosdyke, her cocoa-sprayed outfit forgotten, was shaking her head as though she would never stop.

"Never in my born days," she said. "I never in all my life . . . never would've believed . . . never . . . never . . . never . . ."

Her utterance sounded really quite poetic (in the manner of Tennyson) if a trifle repetitious.

"Oh, what a relief!" Mrs Bagthorpe clasped her hands.

"I'm off to bed," Mr Bagthorpe informed everyone, and left. Other people being bedded down in wardrobes and boilers at least made his own sleeping arrangements seem marginally more attractive.

Jack collected his own sleeping things and went back outside. There he made himself as comfortable as possible by the wardrobe. He lay there, and saw the lights of Ty Cilion Duon go off, one by one. Then he lay and looked up at the stars, and thought how peaceful everything seemed.

"There *is* such a thing as peace," he thought.

He was just about to drift off into sleep when he heard a sound, somewhere to his right. In a moment he was wide-eyed and straining his ears. There it was again! Footsteps, he guessed, on the stones of the drive. Cautiously he lifted his head.

There, moving across the faintly moonlit front of the house, was a dark figure. Breath held, Jack

142

watched. The figure moved very slowly and heavily. It was limping.

Jack nearly yelped aloud with terror. He put out his hand and tried to shake Zero, who merely grunted, and rearranged his head between his paws.

"I'm s-seeing one!" Jack thought. "A g-ghost from the B-Black Corners! It's the Old M-M-Man Limping!"

He clenched his jaw to stop his teeth from chattering. He did not feel that he could bear it if that slow, limping figure should change its course, and advance towards where he lay. So he closed his eyes, tight.

When he opened them again, a long time afterwards, the figure had vanished.

Eleven

When Jack woke up the next morning the wardrobe was empty and Zero had gone. He woke, putting out a hand as usual, expecting to encounter Zero's coat, but found only cold pebbles. This reminder of where he was stirred him into action. He got up and blinked about him. The door of the wardrobe hung wide open, revealing only a dead wolf. Of Zero and Daisy there was no sign.

"They'll have gone into the house," Jack told himself, struggling to his feet. "For breakfast."

The house, however, seemed uncannily quiet for somewhere containing the Bagthorpes, and the sunshine had a thinned, early-morning look. Jack looked at his wristwatch and groaned. Five thirty-five. It looked as though another long day lay ahead.

He heaved a sigh and made towards the house, then stopped dead.

"The Old Man Limping!"

Could it be that there was a connection between Jack's sighting of the night before and the present disappearances? Could Daisy and Zero have been spirited away? Daisy, after all, was a notoriously early riser. On the other hand, Zero was a one-man dog (or so Jack liked to think. The truth was that he would pad amiably along behind almost anybody, except Mr Bagthorpe.) And if Daisy and Zero had been spirited away, why had he himself been left? A sudden thought struck him.

"What if I *have* been? What if I *am* invisible, to everyone else?" He looked down at himself in alarm. He *seemed* to be all there. He gave the back of his hand a little testing pinch.

"Felt that, all right."

He was relieved. Nevertheless, the seeds of doubt had been sown. He did not feel that he would be entirely at ease until he had been sighted by some other human being. He realized that he would have to wait some time for this confirmation of his existence. The whole Bagthorpe tribe was flat out in bed (or boiler).

Jack decided to fry bacon and egg.

"I'll be able to think better when I'm not hungry," he thought.

This he accordingly did. There did not appear to be enough bacon or eggs to provide the entire ménage with a similar breakfast, but this did not deter him.

"The early bird catches the worm," he thought.

As he was assembling his ingredients Zero reappeared. He padded in through the back door, tail wagging.

"*There* you are!" Jack said. "Good boy. Good old chap!"

He had not really believed that anybody would dognap Zero, but was relieved all the same. Daisy, however, did not appear to be with him.

"She'll be all right," he told himself. "She always is."

He set up the stove just outside the house, and lit it. This was the happiest time he had spent in Wales so far. The fresh early-morning smells and whistling of birds combined to give the feeling that God was in his heaven, and all right with the world. (One never normally had this impression in the vicinity of the Bagthorpes.)

Jack sat under a tree and had just begun to tuck in when Rosie appeared, blinking owlishly.

"Hello," she greeted him. "Is it morning? I think the smell of bacon woke me up."

"If you want some, I should grab some quick," he advised her. "There isn't all that much. Was it comfortable in the boiler?"

"Oh Jack!" Rosie's face started to crumple. "What about darling little Daisy? Did you find her?"

"Well, we did," he told her. "Zero did, as a matter of fact. He sniffed her out."

"Oh clever old Zero!" Rosie cried. She ran to him and patted him warmly. "You're a good, clever boy! Give him some bacon, Jack. Where was she?"

"In the wardrobe, as a matter of fact," he replied.

"But there aren't any ward—oh! What—the one Father bought?"

He nodded, mouth full of egg and fried bread.

"Oh, the clever little thing!" Rosie said. "What a good idea!"

Jack swallowed his mouthful.

"The only thing is," he said, "that she's gone again."

"Back up to the castle, you mean?"

"No—at least, I shouldn't think so. She spent the night in the wardrobe, you see, and me and Zero guarded her. She'd gone when I woke up."

"You mean thing!" Rosie was all at once mad and spitting. "You're mean! You're rotten! You're sitting

146

there stuffing yourself with bacon and egg when poor
little Daisy's lost! I'm going to find her!"

She ran off.

"And you were meant to be guarding her!" she
shouted back over her shoulder. "You and that stupid
pudding-headed dog!"

"She means pudding-footed," Jack told Zero.
"Take no notice of her."

He wiped his plate clean with the rest of the bread
and got to his feet. At that point, he heard a horrible,
eerie wailing. It seemed to be coming from the house.

"Good grief!" He stood stock-still, listening.
"Could it. . . ? The wailing Blue Light. . . ? But it's
broad daylight!"

Cautiously he advanced towards the house, followed by Zero, whose fur, Jack was relieved to see,
did not appear to be standing up on end, at least, not
more than usual. It was as he entered the kitchen that
he realized what the sound was.

Grandma had now risen, and seeing no reason why
the rest of the household should slumber on, was
playing one of her records as reveille. William had
mended her plug, but the needle had now stuck. It
was horrible. Even as Jack went through into the hall
Grandma turned the volume up full.

"Good morning, dear child!" she shrieked above
the cacophony.

"Good morning, Grandma. Don't you think you
should turn that down? Father'll go spare."

"I care not a fig," she returned. "It is never too late
to educate oneself, or one's children. We shall all
come to know and love such music."

Jack doubted this, but wisely refrained from saying

147

so. Arguing with Grandma was not easy at the best of times, and against the present racket would be hopeless.

"I'll make you a cup of tea," he told her cunningly. If he could divert her into the kitchen she might forget to put on any more records, and the day might yet be saved.

It was too late. Even above the frantic warblings of Desdemona Jack heard the scream of brakes that could only herald the arrival of Uncle Parker.

"*Now* what?" he wondered.

If Uncle Parker was abroad at this unearthly hour of the morning, it could only mean trouble. Uncle Parker never appeared in public before nine o'clock at the earliest. It was all part of his image as a laid-back man of leisure.

Jack went out to investigate. Uncle Parker was already out of his car and staring at the wardrobe, empty save for the dead wolf (or skunk). He turned as Jack approached. He looked distinctly pale. There even appeared to be rings under his eyes.

"What's up, Uncle Park?"

He shook his head wearily.

"It's that goat. It's that miserable puddling goat."

Something serious was evidently up. Uncle Parker usually left the descriptions of Daisy's goat to Mr Bagthorpe. He himself sometimes even pretended he was quite fond of it.

"What about it?"

"It's been shot."

"*Shot*? What—you mean with a gun?"

Uncle Parker nodded.

"Apparently."

"But—but he *can't* have been! You can't just go

round shooting goats! This is England—well, Wales, anyway."

"Nevertheless," Uncle Parker told him, "someone has thought fit to put a bullet in the brute. One often felt like doing so oneself, of course."

"Is it—*dead*, then?" Jack asked, awestruck by this bloody development.

"Didn't get any details," Uncle Parker said. "I've been up half the night trying to calm Celia. She is in despair."

"She would be," Jack agreed sympathetically. "Anyone would be. After all, he was only a harmless pet."

He realized that this description of Billy Goat Gruff was not strictly accurate, but knew that one should not speak ill of the dead.

"*Now* what, for crying out loud?" came a bellow from the house. Mr Bagthorpe, still in his dressing-gown, stood on the steps. He looked extremely bleary-eyed and bad-tempered.

"Why must you be everlastingly on my doorstep?" he bawled. "Even at *dawn* you hound me."

"It's an emergency," Jack called. "The goat's been shot."

There followed what would have been a silence, but for the caterwauling of the Vienna State Opera Company. Slowly Mr Bagthorpe advanced.

"What?" he croaked. "*What* did you say?"

"Billy Goat Gruff's been shot," Jack repeated. "It's terrible. It's against the law."

"It's a miracle!" exclaimed Mr Bagthorpe in awed tones. "I used not to believe in them. If this is true, I may become a convert. Is it true?"

They both nodded.

"Who did it?" Mr Bagthorpe demanded. "Whoever did it should get a decoration. The MC or the SDP or MBE, or something. How's your terrible daughter taken it?"

His eye fell on the vacant wardrobe.

"Don't tell me," he said slowly, "don't tell me *she*'s been shot, as well? A double!"

"Don't be rotten, Father," Jack told him.

"And that, of course, would eliminate Arry Awk at a stroke," continued Mr Bagthorpe. "By George, a *triple*! Lead me to the shooter, I wish to shake him by the hand."

"What shooter is this?" inquired Mrs Bagthorpe, emerging in a state of considerable dishabille. "What are you talking about?"

Briefly Jack filled her in.

"Oh dear—whatever shall we do?" cried Mrs Bagthorpe. She usually did a good twenty minutes' Yoga and Deep Breathing first thing in the morning before emerging to face the world in general, and her own family in particular. "What shall we do?" she repeated desperately.

"Hang out the flags?" suggested her husband. "Crack the champagne, sound—"

150

"Does dearest Celia know?" she interrupted.

"She does," replied Uncle Parker briefly. "Those damfool police went up there and told her last night. Then, frightened by what they had done, they came down here and fetched me, you'll remember. I shall sue them."

He probably would, too, Jack reflected. Aunt Celia was, quite unaccountably, the light of his life.

"Perhaps I should go up and try to calm her," Mrs Bagthorpe said worriedly.

"You do that," said her husband. "And take that contraption of Mother's with you. That'll calm her. *That*'ll kill or cure! Ha!"

He was now in high good humour.

"Where is my daughter?" demanded Uncle Parker, taking the offensive. "She was left in your charge."

"Zero and me guarded her," Jack told him unhappily. "I woke up and they'd both gone – her and Zero. I thought they'd gone on a Dragon Hunt. I'm sorry, I really am."

"There is no need to take the blame upon yourself, dear child." Grandma, who had evidently been listening unobserved, now put her oar in. "You are a minor, and in the care of your father. He must be held responsible."

"This, Mother, is one Can I shall not Carry," he told her. "I expect the law has its own penalties for those who leave infants in wardrobes."

"There is one thing . . ." Jack said. "Last night, when you'd all gone to bed . . . well, someone came."

"Like who?" demanded his father.

"I – I don't know," Jack admitted. "It was definitely a man. He seemed to sort of come and go."

"For crying out loud!" exclaimed Mr Bagthorpe. "If you've got something to say, say it. Spit it out!"

"I think . . . I think it was the Old Man Limping," Jack said.

"Oh Jack, do you really?" cried Mrs Bagthorpe. "How dreadful for you, out here all on your own!"

"It wasn't too bad," said Jack, grateful nonetheless for the sympathy. "The only thing is, he had footsteps – I mean ones that you could actually hear. *Would* a ghost have footsteps?"

"Of course it would," Mr Bagthorpe told him. "They can bang and rattle like merry hell if they want. What did it look like? Did it have a greenish-white face, or what?"

Jack was tempted to say that it had, but honesty prevailed.

"I didn't exactly see," he admitted. "I sort of had my eyes half closed."

"Ye gods!" said Mr Bagthorpe disgustedly. "I pay an extortionate rent for a place with fewer amenities than Dotheboys Hall, expressly for the chance to encounter a ghost, and the first one that turns up, you had your eyes shut! If only I had –"

"Coo-eee! Coo-ee!" came a familiar, high-pitched voice. Daisy Parker came trotting out of the undergrowth, the state of her person and clothing seeming to suggest that she had been on an all-night Assault Course.

"Here we are," she told them. "We had a lovely time!"

Nobody much liked the sound of this. In the first place, the use of the first person plural would seem to suggest that Arry Awk was in the offing. In the second, when Daisy had a lovely time, it usually boded ill for everyone else.

"We been playing Little Bo Peep," she announced happily.

So she had, it later emerged – with a vengeance.

"Such innocence, such joy!" murmured Grandma.

"Oh, there you are, Daisy!" said her father, with manifest relief. He had himself felt certain that she would turn up alive and kicking, but had doubted whether Aunt Celia, in her present state, could be convinced of this.

"I'se hungry," Daisy announced. "And Arry Awk. He's hungry as well. He says he want to gobble 'n gobble 'n gobble!"

"Just hop in," her parent told her, indicating his car. "We'll have you fed in no time."

Daisy shook her head vigorously. Her tangled ringlets flew.

"I not coming," she stated. "I want to stop."

"There's no breakfast here," Jack told her. "There's nothing to eat."

"Nonsense," said Grandma. "Of course there is. You shall have my own share, dear child."

"You keep out of this," Mr Bagthorpe told her. He was often ruder to his mother than anybody else since Hamlet. "Tell her about her devilish goat, Russell."

Uncle Parker hesitated. He had been going to wait for what seemed a suitable opportunity for this, but now realized that it was probably the only way he would winkle her out of the Bagthorpe ménage, short of using brute force.

"Billy Goat Gruff!" squealed Daisy joyously. "You *found* him! Oh, clever, clever Daddy!"

"Well – not exactly," said her unfortunate parent. Jack felt really sorry for him. He already had Aunt Celia in a state of derangement on his hands. Soon he would have a hysterical Daisy as well.

"Where is he?" she continued. "I want to see him an' cuddle him! Oh, my darling lickle Billy!"

Now Jack felt sorry for her, too.

"Well, the fact is, Daisy," Uncle Parker began, "that Billy Goat Gruff –" he hesitated.

"He's been shot," supplied Mr Bagthorpe starkly. "He's been shot dead."

"Not necessarily," put in Jack quickly. "You can be shot without being dead."

Daisy meanwhile stood with mouth open and eyes stretched. (She had very big, as well as very sharp, eyes.)

"Shotted with a *gun*?" she squeaked disbelievingly.

"'Fraid so, Daisy," Uncle Parker told her miserably.

"I don't mind forking out for flowers," said Mr Bagthorpe. "Ha!"

154

Daisy let out a cry of anguish and ran to Grandma, who held her closely.

"There, there, my darling," she said. "Never mind—you still have me."

Judging by her sobs and wails Daisy found this cold comfort.

"Let us go and find Thomas the Second," Grandma suggested. "There are many new tricks he can yet learn."

"Look, Grandma," said Uncle Parker, "I can't go back up there without Daisy, you know. Her mother is beside herself."

"As ever," said Mr Bagthorpe, not particularly sotto voce.

"It is a pity," said Grandma, "that my only daughter should be so wishy-washy. It is a mystery how she managed to produce a child as vibrant as Daisy."

She had to speak very loudly in order to be heard above the shrieks of that vibrant child.

"You will simply have to pick her up and take her, Russell," Mrs Bagthorpe told him desperately. "I will accompany you. I may be able to calm poor Celia."

"I'll come as well," Jack volunteered. "Then I could run back here with messages, with there being no 'phone."

He had already eaten breakfast, but felt that he would be able to manage another quite shortly.

"How sensible, Jack!" exclaimed Mrs Bagthorpe warmly.

Uncle Parker braced himself, strode resolutely forward and extricated a screaming and kicking Daisy from Grandma's embrace. There was no way anybody could do this while at the same time appearing nonchalant and cool, and Mr Bagthorpe watched the operation with ill-concealed delight.

"Mind she doesn't bite, Russell," he advised. "Now, at last, you are reaping what you have sown."

He made Daisy sound like a rabid ear of corn.

Jack climbed into the tiny seat at the rear of the roadster. Mrs Bagthorpe sat in the front, and the squirming Daisy was deposited on her lap. Uncle Parker jumped into the driving seat, slammed the door, and revved noisily. The car leapt forward, and in the same moment there was a scream of brakes and it came to an abrupt, bucking halt. Inches away from it was another car (though not one belonging to the police). As the Bagthorpes watched, dazed, a man climbed out and advanced menacingly.

"You Parker?" he snarled.

Jack watched him, stunned. The man was not particularly Old – but he was definitely Limping!

Twelve

"Who're you?" demanded Uncle Parker. "And what the blazes are you doing driving at ninety miles per hour in a private drive?"

"Jones," replied the other. "And there are plenty of witnesses to testify to my speed, which was twenty, approximately."

He looked expectantly at his audience, and was met by stony stares. By now heads were poking out of upstairs windows.

"You were going much too fast!" shouted William. "Uncle Park had only just started his engine."

All the younger Bagthorpes were fond of their uncle, and at present he was also, of course, the provider of sunken baths, and good food.

"The way 'e goes 'urtling and 'ooting about is a disgrace," Mrs Fosdyke appearing on the steps, treacherously testified.

Mr Bagthorpe was himself torn between the desire to see Uncle Parker shot down in flames and his pathological hatred of visitors.

"What are you doing here?" he demanded rudely. "No tradesmen or hawkers or circulars or charity collectors."

He was quoting the notice to this effect on the gate of Unicorn House.

"You Bagthorpe?" asked the visitor.

"Clear off, Jones," returned Mr Bagthorpe. "Is *everybody* in this benighted country called Jones?"

There was a noisy revving and a shower of stones. Uncle Parker had taken advantage of the diversion to steer his car round that of the visitor, and was hurtling back up to the castle and his deranged wife.

"Hey, stop!" yelled Mr Jones.

He ran back to his own vehicle, executed a three-point turn, and drove off in pursuit. Mr Bagthorpe, who had been looking forward to a thoroughgoing slanging match, was clearly disappointed by this.

"Get his number!" he yelled.

This instruction fell on deaf ears.

Jack was used to Uncle Parker's driving, but on this occasion did what the majority of his other passengers did, and closed his eyes. Daisy was still squirming and sobbing on Mrs Bagthorpe's lap.

When they reached the castle Uncle Parker scooped her up and strode inside, followed by the others. It was only then, in the lobby, with its potted palms and chandeliers, that Mrs Bagthorpe realized that her hair was still in plaits and that she was wearing her nightdress. It was one that Aunt Penelope had made, and given her for Christmas. It was, as Mr Bagthorpe had remarked when his wife unwrapped it, the last word in frumpishness.

"There again," he had said, "if she had her way, she would dress the entire female populace to resemble Mrs Squeers. It would reduce the occasions of sin. Pray do not wear that garment in *my* sight."

It was the expression on the receptionist's face that alerted Mrs Bagthorpe to her plight.

"Oh dear!" she gasped, realizing in a flash that the violet fur-edged slippers that had been Mrs Fosdyke's Christmas gift put paid to any chance that she might carry off the occasion with an air.

The receptionist, who had a *coiffure* rather than hair, and long, blood-red nails, wore the expression of one who has discovered a slug in her salad.

"If a man called Jones asks for me," Uncle Parker told her, "tell him I'm out. Tell him I've gone fishing, or to an Eisteddfod, or something."

"Yes, sir," said that bewildered lady. "And what if the police come again?"

"Tell 'em the same," he said, and followed Mrs Bagthorpe, who was moving very fast indeed in the direction of the lift.

When the party arrived at Uncle Parker's suite, it was to discover Aunt Celia, in ivory, lace-trimmed satin, pacing up and down and wringing her hands and giving a fair impression of the Lady of Shalott. Mrs Bagthorpe tried to embrace her, and Aunt Celia herself attempted to embrace Daisy, but nobody really succeeded.

"Oh, the cruelty of Man!" cried Aunt Celia despairingly. "Man's inhumanity to Man – and goats! My heart is pierced, the iron has entered my soul!"

This, Jack thought, sounded fairly serious. He knew that she was vegetarian, and anti-Blood Sports, but had not guessed how passionately she would react to Billy Goat Gruff's demise.

"He obviously *is* dead, not just winged," he thought, "or she wouldn't be carrying on like this."

159

"All life is sacred," she declared, "even the meanest beast of the field."

"Of course it is, dearest," said Uncle Parker soothingly.

"I want my lickle Billy!" Daisy was wailing non-stop.

"I think you should get another goat immediately, Russell," Mrs Bagthorpe told him. "Just as one must always go straight up in another aeroplane, when one has crashed. After all, all goats are the same under the skin."

She was beginning to sound just like Aunt Celia.

The telephone rang. Uncle Parker picked it up.

"*What?*" he exclaimed. "Where? Speak up!"

He was having difficulty in hearing his caller above the racket being made by his female relatives.

"Look," Jack heard him say, "either he is, or he isn't. Are you mad, or blind, or what?"

The conversation went on for quite a long time, and in the end Uncle Parker said, "I'll be right over," and rang off.

"That was the police," he said, though only Jack was listening properly. "They say they've got the goat down at the station."

"His body, you mean?" Jack asked.

"Alive and kicking, according to them," Uncle Parker replied. He seemed dazed.

It took some time to get this information through to Aunt Celia and Daisy, but when at last they did grasp it, their reactions were ecstatic.

"My prayers have been answered!" cried Aunt Celia, clasping her hands.

This remark seemed to indicate that she believed Billy Goat Gruff to have been literally resurrected.

160

"Even *she* can't believe that!" Jack thought, though without conviction.

"My tears are now of purest joy!" she told everyone.

Tears were, in fact, pouring down her cheeks, and Jack thought, not for the first time, how amazing it was that she should be able to cry, sometimes for hours on end, and still look beautiful. Most people went blotchy, their eyes puffed up and their noses went red. On the other hand, he reflected, perhaps weeping was different from crying, and Aunt Celia definitely wept.

"Oh my funny lickly Billy!" squealed Daisy. "I'se going to get him a million lickle bells and tassels all over!"

"That's the spirit, Daisy!" said her relieved father.

At this point there came a hammering, rather than a knocking, at the door. Daisy scooted over and opened it to reveal the Mr Jones they had encountered earlier.

"Right, Parker!" he said grimly. "Let's get down to business, shall we?"

"What business is that, exactly?" queried Uncle Parker coolly.

"Damages," replied Mr Jones. "That's what."

The tale that then unfolded was complicated, but the gist of it was that it had been Mr Jones's goat, and not Daisy's, that had been shot. The inhabitants of Llosilli were all in a state of jumpiness after the happenings of the previous day. Some trigger-happy person, sighting a goat in the dusk, had shot it.

"Then you must go after the shooter," Uncle Parker told his visitor. "It's no affair of mine."

161

"He shot it in good faith," returned Mr Jones. "He thought it was *your* crazy animal."

"Then he made a mistake," Uncle Parker told him. "Though I cannot think why. You do not, I take it, get *your* goat up in bells and ribbons?"

Mr Jones did not reply. His mouth opened, but nothing came out. Judging by his expression he was seeing a vision over Uncle Parker's left shoulder. Jack followed the line of his gaze.

"So *that*'s it!" he thought, enlightened.

Quite often in the past he had seen men react like this to the sight of Aunt Celia. They were like hypnotized rabbits.

"Oh, Mr Jones," she cooed, advancing toward him, "how can I ever thank you?"

Mr Jones now looked somewhat like a fish, eyes bulging and mouth silently opening and shutting.

"You have restored my happiness," she continued, and, leaning forward, placed a light kiss on his cheek.

Jack himself knew that this meant nothing. If Aunt Celia was in a kissing mood, she would kiss anything that moved, even policemen. Mr Jones, of course, was not to know this. He looked as if he might be going to faint.

"There we are!" said Uncle Parker, capitalizing on his wife's effect. "So that's all settled nicely. Care for a drink? Rather early in the day, I grant, but a Buck's Fizz wouldn't come amiss."

He accordingly rang Room Service and ordered this. Mr Jones said that he was teetotal, but would not say no to an orange juice, and soon the party was sitting around in a considerable state of euphoria. Mrs Bagthorpe in particular became extremely giggly. She said that nothing would induce her to go past the *coiffure* in the reception again in her nightie, and she and Aunt Celia retired to the bedroom so that she could try on clothes for something suitable to borrow.

When she reappeared she was wearing Aunt Celia's waterfall outfit. Mrs Bagthorpe was of quite different proportions from her willowy sister-in-law, and looked like something rather more substantial than a cascading Welsh cataract – Niagara, for instance.

It was then decided that in view of Uncle Parker's consumption of Buck's Fizz, Mr Jones should drive him and Daisy down to the police station, first dropping off Jack and his mother at Ty Cilion Duon.

"And you must dine with us tonight," Uncle Parker told him. "Mustn't he, Celia?"

"Certainly you must, Mr Jones," she murmured. "Or shall I call you. . . ?"

"Dai," he supplied.

Jack stiffened for a moment, then relaxed. Wales must be full of Dai Joneses.

It was clear from the existing state of *bonhomie* that all prosecutions regarding the shooting of the goat were to be dropped.

"Mangy old beast, it was," Mr Jones confided during the drive down. "And only a flesh wound, anyhow."

Uncle Parker then magnaminously offered to pay the vet's fee, but this was waved aside. Jack thought that he could now understand what Uncle Parker saw in Aunt Celia. She must be worth her weight in gold, he reflected.

He and his mother were dropped off at the end of the drive to Ty Cilion Duon.

"Do you know, I think I may be going to enjoy this holiday, after all," Mrs Bagthorpe told Jack.

She was tripping left and right over her waterfall (she was shorter than Aunt Celia, as well as stouter) but seemed not to mind in the least. In one hand she gaily swung the plastic carrier containing her shed nightdress. All of a sudden, to Jack's astonishment, she gave this a brief, but vigorous, whirl, as if preparing to toss the caber, and flung it far into the shrubbery.

"Ooops!" she cried. "Gone for ever, hateful garment!"

"Mother!" remonstrated Jack, and started forward to retrieve it.

"Leave it!" she commanded. "I do not want my gesture spoilt!"

She gave a couple of unsteady skips, then added,

"You may, perhaps, pick it up later. But only to avoid litter. Put it straight into the dustbin." (Ty Cilion Duon did have a dustbin, in fact, it had three. Refuse collection was the only department in which it was well furnished.)

"Are you sure?" Jack asked. "Aunt Penelope made it specially for you, remember."

"Fiddle Penelope!" cried Mrs Bagthorpe. "She made it like that on purpose, to spoil our marriage!"

It seemed odd to Jack to hear his mother being carefree and uncharitable in the same breath.

"That Buck's Fizz certainly bucked her up!" he thought.

"I only kept it to annoy your father," she now confided. She giggled. "It was like a red rag to a bull. It was one of my weapons!"

Jack felt that he was seeing his mother in an entirely new light. Heretofore he had believed that she coped with life in general and Mr Bagthorpe in particular by dint of Breathing and Yoga and Positive Thinking. It now appeared that her mind really worked along much the same lines as everyone else's. He wondered what the readers would think of Stella Bright if they could see her at this moment.

They now rounded the last bend in the drive. Jack could see his father ahead, standing by the wardrobe. He was evidently considering what to charge Grandma for the axe damage, or weighing up its possibilities for conversion into a detached dwelling.

"Henry!" called Mrs Bagthorpe. "Cooee!"

She started forward at as near a canter as Niagara would allow. Mr Bagthorpe turned and Jack saw his incredulous stare. Then, on the last lap, she tripped and fell. She did not get to her feet immediately. Jack thought this was because she had hurt herself, but when he reached her, realized that she was just lying there, resting. She was gazing up at the sky and smiling.

"What the blazes is going on?" demanded Mr Bagthorpe. He strode across and stood over her. Her gaze moved, but she did not.

"Henry . . ." she murmured, in a style reminiscent of a Mills and Boon heroine on the last page.

"Get up, Laura!" he ordered. "And wipe that silly smile off your face!"

Mr Bagthorpe was not, and never had been, a reader of Mills and Boon. He had never even sat through *Gone With The Wind* to the end, let alone *Brief Encounter*. In all the TV scripts he had written, there had not been a single love scene.

"What's that you've got on?" he continued. "Get *up*, Laura!"

He did not offer her a hand, so Jack did. She rose

166

heavily and clumsily to her feet. If she had hoped to bring out the latent romantic in her husband by donning Aunt Celia's robe and ditching Aunt Penelope's, she was disappointed.

"Good grief!" he exclaimed, eyeing her up and down. "It's that fancy dress of Celia's! Take it off at once. If there is one thing I detest, it is mutton dressed as lamb!"

As Mrs Bagthorpe stood there, smiling sweetly, Jack could have sworn that he saw her eyes narrow.

"There is splendid news, Henry," she told him. "Dearest Daisy's darling goat is *not* shot, after all! Isn't that good news?"

She knew perfectly well that it was not – for anyone but Daisy and her mother. It had the desired effect. Mr Bagthorpe's reaction to this intelligence was less than euphoric.

"Is *what*?" he said. "Not shot?"

"Not shot," repeated Mrs Bagthorpe. "We have been having a lovely celebration up at the castle, with that nice Mr Jones."

"They had Buck's Fizz," Jack put in, thinking to enlighten his father about Mrs Bagthorpe's own state of dreamy happiness.

"Ye gods!" he said bitterly. "My own wife and helpmeet! It is bad enough having my own mother polluting the airwaves with a tribe of hysterical hyenas like a snake in the grass. We now have a wooden horse within the walls. Did you get your thirty pieces of silver?"

On he ranted, mixing his metaphors as never before. He had come to Wales, he said, to carry out serious, scientific research. He had not yet seen a single ghost, all he had was cuckoos in the nest and blacklegs.

"Anyone with an ordinary job," he ended morosely, "can resign. When they're fed up, they just hand in their cards. As a sensitive creative writer, I have no escape. I haven't even got a card to *hand* in.'"

"Oh Henry!" cried his wife when he had finished. "How *seriously* you take everything! Forget your work, forget dull care! Take a holiday – come revel with the rest of us!"

There was a silence while Mr Bagthorpe took a grip of himself.

"If this is a revel," he said at last between gritted teeth, "then I am Marco de Polo!"

"Marco Polo, you mean," said Jack who, as one being constantly corrected himself, was pleased to have this rare opportunity to correct somebody else. He should have known better.

"I mean no one of the kind," snapped Mr Bagthorpe. "I mean Marco de Polo. The fellow who invented America."

"I think you're mixing him up with Vasco da Gama, Father," Jack unwisely persisted.

"I am doing nothing of the sort," Mr Bagthorpe told him. "Nor am I mixing him up with Guy de Maupassant, or Charles de Gaulle!"

Jack shrugged and let the matter drop. Trying to correct Mr Bagthorpe was like trying to nail jelly to the ceiling. Mrs Bagthorpe shrugged too, and turned towards the house. Further communication with her husband seemed hopeless. Between them yawned the chasm that divides those who have consumed champagne before breakfast from those who have not.

168

"The day still lies before us, full of promise," Jack heard her say sadly, to herself. It was probably something she repeated every day when she woke, to give her the strength to get up. She seemed all at once deflated, the fizz had gone out of her. Jack felt sorry for her. She had seemed so happy and girlish only minutes before. He felt correspondingly fed up with his father.

"I really like it here," he told him. "We all do. Thanks for bringing us. Especially now we know it's not haunted."

He entered the house, feeling as he did so Mr Bagthorpe's murderous glare boring between his shoulder-blades. He crossed the hall into the sitting-room, put another record on, and turned the volume up full.

Thirteen

The Bagthorpes were in the middle of breakfast when the first sheep appeared. (Later, there was to be a whole flock.) They were not having much of a meal, partly because the process of cooking things on a camping stove was extremely tedious, and partly because there were insufficient provisions for everybody.

Just before the first sitting was about to pick up their knives and forks, Rosie reappeared in a dishevelled and tearful state, having spent a full two hours fruitlessly searching for Daisy. When told that Daisy was safe she was ecstatic, and when she heard that Billy Goat Gruff was also alive and well, albeit in police custody, her joy was extreme.

"Oh darling little Billy!" she cried, sounding exactly like Daisy herself. "I love him, he's sweet."

She looked around her at her unsmiling relatives.

"I think you all do, really," she continued. "You just *pretend* not to, like with Zero."

This was a serious misjudgement. Several people present, notably Mr Bagthorpe and Mrs Fosdyke, actively hated the goat. The rest merely detested it.

"If them Welsh police 'as any sense, they'll have

that goat put down, while they've got 'old of it,"
observed Mrs Fosdyke, walloping fried bread on to
the plates. She usually took a pride in presenting her
meals in an artistic and appetising way. She would not
dream, for instance, of serving a salmon mousse other
than in the shape of a fish, with a painstaking overlay
of cucumber slices as scales. At Ty Cilion Duon she
had lost all heart for this, and just scraped and
shovelled the food around. (Also, of course, there was
no salmon mousse.)

"Rosie, darling, you must be famished!" Mrs
Bagthorpe said, chiefly to avert yet another heated
debate about the goat. She had changed from the
waterfall into an old Indian cotton, and seemed more
or less herself again. "She had better have your
portion, Henry. You can wait for the second sitting."

"There ain't no second sitting," Mrs Fosdyke
informed her. "There's nothing left. There's no
bacon, no sausage, no eggs, no mushrooms, no
tomatoes, no nothing. There's bread and marge for
them that wants it."

"Ye' gods!" exclaimed Mr Bagthorpe. "*I'll* have
that plate, Laura. Unlike the rest of you, I am trying to
work."

"Nonsense, Henry," his wife said. "The less you
eat, the more active your brain becomes. George
Bernard Shaw knew this well. Have some bread and
marge, and an apple."

"I am also," he continued, "engaged in a deadly
battle with this fellow Jones, not to mention that
damned resurrected goat and half Wales besides. An
army marches on its stomach, Laura."

"How you do exaggerate," she replied. "In any

case, you are a middle-aged man, while Rosie is a growing child. Here, Rosie dear, get started before it is cold."

She whipped the plate from under his nose. The slight emphasis she had placed on the word 'middle-aged' indicated that she was actually in the business of paying him out for his earlier remarks, rather than feeding a growing child.

"I have been thinking," Mrs Bagthorpe went on, as she distributed bread to the less fortunate of her family, "we really must try to establish some kind of order in our lives. We may be on holiday, but—"

She got no further. There was a shriek from Mrs Fosdyke, who dropped the frying pan, scooted across the room into the hall and banged the door. The first sheep had arrived.

It stood just inside the back door, looking calmly about and chewing thoughtfully. The Bagthorpes looked back at it, momentarily floored. They were probably less taken aback than most other families would have been, used as they were to the presence in the house of Billy Goat Gruff. Nonetheless, this visitor had arrived unannounced, and they were startled.

"That's not Billy!" said Jack unnecessarily.

Zero, who was slumped by his feet, exhausted by his early-morning exercise, lifted his head and saw the intruder. He then got up, padded over and sniffed at it, wagging his tail.

"Just look at that!" said Mr Bagthorpe. "It could've been a wild boar, or a man-eating tiger!"

Mrs Bagthorpe took a little run at it and clapped her hands.

"Shoo!" she cried.

The sheep ignored her.

"*That* told it, Laura!" said her husband with heavy sarcasm.

"It—it is probably a cade lamb," she replied defensively, "and quite accustomed to being part of a household."

"Well, it's not stopping in *this* one," said Mr Bagthorpe decisively. "It's to be hoped to God it's not the leader, and got the whole *pack* of 'em out there."

"Flock, Henry," Grandma corrected him. "The word is flock. A child of four would have known that."

"Your record's run down," he returned. "Go and put it on again. *That*'ll see it off, cade or not."

The inner door opened cautiously and Mrs Fosdyke's head appeared.

"'As it gone?" she inquired. "Oooh—it ain't!"

"At least it won't charge or kill," Mr Bagthorpe said. "Nobody need hide, or stand on their chairs. It is only a piece of harmless mutton."

"There's sheep," uttered Mrs Fosdyke lugubriously, "and there's sheep. *And* there's wolfs in sheep's waistcoats."

"We could always kill it and have it for dinner," William suggested. "Quite interesting, that—wolf with mint sauce. You don't see it a lot on menus."

At this point there came a faint but distinct bleat. It sounded quite far away.

"That's funny," Jack said. "It never moved its mouth. I was watching it."

They all looked at the sheep. After a few moments there came another baa—nearer, this time, but still

173

quite far away. The sheep appeared to be chewing at the time. The Bagthorpes looked at one another askance. Could the sheep, they wondered, be a ventriloquist? A gifted one, at that.

As they watched in wild surmise, the door nudged open further and a second sheep appeared.

"Oh my God!" said Mr Bagthorpe. "The whole pack *is* out there!"

This sheep appeared to be a more outgoing personality than the other. It wandered round inspecting its surroundings, and went nudging and bumbling about between the deckchairs, whose occupants eyed it warily.

"Shoo it out, somebody!" ordered Mr Bagthorpe who, despite his earlier pronouncement about the harmlessness of mutton, had his own feet tucked well in. "Shoo 'em both out!"

"I think it's sweet," said Rosie, through a mouthful of bacon and egg. "They both are. We could keep them as pets. Then we could shear them and card the wool, and I could take up Spinning as another String to my Bow."

"'Ow do we know they don't belong that Daisy Parker?" said Mrs Fosdyke's head. "'Ow do we know they ain't got 'er a 'ole flock of sheep, to go with that goat?"

"And if so, how very apt," Grandma remarked, "Pure poetry. Little Bo Peep . . ."

At these last words alarm bells rang in several heads.

"Daisy!" Jack said. "When she got back – that's what she said! She said she'd been playing Little Bo Peep!"

He made for the outer door, thus alarming the first sheep, which lumbered heavily forward, causing Mrs Fosdyke to squeak and slam the door again.

"Crikey! Come and look at this!" Jack called.

The family moved, leaving the two sheep in occupation of the kitchen.

Among the seeding grasses, elders and brambles of the garden of Ty Cilion Duon, further woolly shapes could be descried. From time to time came the occasional contented bleat. For a while the Bagthorpes watched this unlikely scene in silence. Then, "Round 'em up!" Mr Bagthorpe ordered. "Get that mutton-headed hound to round 'em up!"

Zero showed not the slightest inclination to do this. He sat at Jack's feet, taking in the scene with everybody else. He had already met two sheep, and had now lost interest. He actually yawned. This infuriated Mr Bagthorpe (not least because it reminded him of his own expensive yawns of the previous day).

"Look at that!" he yelled. "The whole garden is being destroyed by a pack of ravening sheep, and he sits there yawning like Rip Van Winkie!"

"Winkle, or Wee Willie?" murmured William.

"What garden, Henry?" said Grandma. "One would scarcely describe this as a garden. The sheep are doing Mr Jones a service."

"Zero's not meant to be a sheepdog," Jack said. "If he went after the sheep, that'd mean he was a sheep-worrier. And he's not one of those, either. He's anti-Blood Sport."

Mr Bagthorpe's brain had been working rapidly since his mother's last remark. It was true, he thought,

175

that if the brutes kept chewing at this rate, the place would soon have a recognizable lawn and shrubbery, for the first time in decades, probably. If that happened, then he could claim that he and his family had brought about this reclamation, and get expenses. Also if, as seemed certain, Daisy Parker had let the sheep out in her rôle as Little Bo Peep, fur would shortly fly. The farmer whose sheep they were would come after them, probably with a gun, and with any luck Uncle Parker would get shot. All in all, this seemed to Mr Bagthorpe a highly desirable state of affairs.

"Come," he said. "Leave them to it. Sheep may safely graze – ha! Hell's bells!" – this last as he turned to re-enter the kitchen and tripped over one of the original sheep, who had evidently found little to nibble in there, and was emerging to safely graze with its fellows.

Jack was not particularly surprised by Mr Bagthorpe's apparent volte face. He thought he could see the way his father's mind was working. Given the fact that a goat had already been shot at, and given the hysterical way the inhabitants of Llosilli had acted the previous day, he too thought it likely that a farmer would soon be on Daisy's track. Unlike his father, Jack had no wish to see Uncle Parker shot.

"You and me'll round them up later, old chap," he told Zero, when the others had gone back inside. He said this with more confidence than he felt. The sheep in the garden were not behaving much like a flock. They were here, there and everywhere. Jack tried twice to count them, and got eleven the first time, and seventeen the next.

"There's another snag, as well," he thought. "Even when we've rounded them up, we don't know where to drive them. We don't know where they're from."

Recent observation had shown that Wales was littered with mountains and fields full of sheep. This problem, however, was solved sooner than he thought. On re-entering the kitchen he found it deserted. Beyond the agonized bellows of Othello he could hear the unmistakable sounds of a first class Row.

He hurried across the luggage-strewn hall and into the porch, to see a Land Rover in the drive, and a small dark man positively dancing with rage. He seemed to be accusing Mr Bagthorpe of being a sheep-rustler.

"Sheep-rustler my elbow!" Mr Bagthorpe was yelling. "Your accursed beasts are destroying my property left and right! They're terrorizing my household. Get 'em rounded up and off my land! And get your fences mended!"

He appeared in the heat of the moment to have forgotten his intention to shop Daisy Parker. Not so Mrs Fosdyke.

"You want to get after that Daisy!" she screeched. "She's roaming all over playing Bo Peep!"

There was a momentary lull after these last words were uttered.

"What?" said the farmer. "What did you say?"

"Daisy Parker," said Mrs Fosdyke smugly, pleased at holding the centre of the stage in so important a scene. "Playing Po Beep."

There was a pause, and a couple of titters.

"Bo Peep," she amended.

The farmer appeared temporarily stumped. All this talk of daisies and Bo Peep had him foxed.

"As a matter of fact," Mr Bagthorpe told him coldly, "you are barking up entirely the wrong tree. Your damned flock's here all right, too true it is—hundreds of 'em—look, look at that brute behind you, damaging my wardrobe!"

The dazed farmer turned and saw the megalithic wardrobe rearing in the drive behind him, and his grasp on reality seemed to slip further.

"The *flock* is here," Mr Bagthorpe continued, "but the rustler is not. Do I *look* like a sheep-rustler, for God's sake? What use do you think *I've* got for a bunch of chewy Welsh mutton? Get that vehicle off my drive and get up the road!"

"Yes, you get up to that castle," Mrs Fosdyke told him. "And make sure you report it to the Welsh police. If they don't lock that Daisy up now, they never will. They've 'ad chance enough, Lord knows. Do you know 'ow many police cars she's crashed? Do you—?"

On and on she rambled. The mystified sheep-farmer was now shaking his head more or less non-stop, as so often people did when brought into confrontation with the Bagthorpe clan.

Mrs Bagthorpe, seeing signs that if Mrs Fosdyke were not silenced soon Rosie would start kicking her shins (she was already yelling "Fibber, fibber, traitor, traitor!" at the top of her voice), now intervened.

"I think I can explain matters, Mr—er. . . ?"

"Jones," said the farmer.

"It would be, wouldn't it?" said Mr Bagthorpe.

"Your sheep, as you can see, Mr Jones," went on

178

Mrs Bagthorpe, "are certainly in our garden. They are not here, however, because of any action of ours, or even at our invitation. It is all rather complicated to explain to an outsider such as yourself, but some relatives of ours are staying at the castle up the road, and they have a rather . . ." here she paused, at a loss as to how exactly to describe Daisy ". . . a rather precocious and original five-year-old."

Here Mr Bagthorpe and Mrs Fosdyke let out concerted snorts of disgust.

"I'm afraid that Daisy does sometimes cause mischief," continued Mrs Bagthorpe, "though quite unwittingly, of course. I gather that she was out this morning playing at Little Bo Peep before breakfast."

The poleaxed Mr Jones was staring at her, speechless.

"She is at an age when there is a very thin line between fantasy and reality," explained Mrs Bagthorpe, now on firmer ground, since she often made this kind of psychological analysis when sitting on the Bench, or being Stella Bright. "She takes her roleplaying into everyday life, you see. It really is quite common at that age."

"It is not all *that* common," put in Grandma, jealous of Daisy's reputation as resident Poet and Genius. "Daisy is quite singular in most respects."

"Amen to that," said her son. "If ever she became plural, it would be the end of civilization as we know it."

"You get straight up to that castle," Mrs Fosdyke advised the visitor. "Before they 'op it."

"I will, yes, indeed," he muttered. "What was their name again? And the *castle* – you're sure, now?"

"Parker," Mr Bagthorpe told him. "Sure. Positive."

179

Mr Jones climbed dumbly into his vehicle and executed a turn.

"Got your American Express?" Mr Bagthorpe shouted after him. "Ha!"

"I suppose you're satisfied now," said Rosie bitterly. "Poor little Daisy."

"Poor Uncle Park, you mean," Jack told her.

"He certainly Carries the Can, in that ménage," agreed Mr Bagthorpe, "just as I do in this. He'll find this Mr Jones rather more difficult to talk round than the other, I think."

"It was Aunt Celia, not him," Jack said. "She might get round this one, as well."

This, it later emerged, was not the case. Farmer Jones was immune to Aunt Celia's charms, and downright disgusted by Daisy and her goat. His first shock on arriving at the castle was to see members of his missing flock adrift on its manicured lawns (not to mention its flower-beds). On entering the foyer he was recognized by a porter, the management was sent for, and he was curtly ordered to remove himself and his sheep forthwith.

"Many of our clients are threatening to leave," the manager told him. "We appear to be under constant surveillance by the police, and now this. Our clients are not the kind of people who expect to rise and look through the window to be confronted by a flock of sheep. I understand that the tennis courts are under occupation, and the croquet lawn. Several hoops have been bent. In the car park, a Daimler has been involved, and a Lotus. When the final bill for damages is drawn up, it will be presented to you. I advise you to consult your solicitor."

The manager stalked off to his quarters. Mr Jones tottered to the reception desk.

"Parker," he croaked. "Stopping here. And a daisy, or something."

The *coiffure* nodded sagely.

"Ah, I *see* . . ."

"You *do*?" said Mr Jones eagerly. He himself could see nothing.

"Oh, yes, indeed," the receptionist told him.

She then proceeded to fill him in. She was probably not supposed to do so. Receptionists are meant to be discreet, and to overlook their clients' little foibles. On the other hand, the mayhem caused by the Parkers (and their relatives) during their short stay had been of an order never before witnessed by this august establishment.

Quite apart from a constant strong police presence, the receptionist told Mr Jones, there had been, initially at least, the goat.

"Puddles everywhere," she told him, "even in the lift. Mr Carruthers had a page on full-time duty with an aerosol deodorant, and a spray of Chanel Number Five."

Then there had been an almost constant procession

of conspicuously unwashed bodies. She went into some detail describing the appearance of William after his boiler-cleaning session, and of the chambermaid's description of the state of the bath towels afterwards.

"We have become virtually a Public Bathhouse," she said. "Imagine! And a Cabinet Minister staying, and a TV star off *Crossroads*!"

As she twittered on Mr Jones was looking about him at the opulence of the foyer, and making certain rapid calculations. He had heard rumours about the grandeur and luxury of the newly-converted castle, and the wealth of its clientèle. He and his wife had almost dined there on their wedding anniversary, and then got cold feet at the last moment. Mrs Jones was not sure whether her new frock would stand up, and they were both nervous about using the wrong cutlery, or the whole menu being in French (it was).

"Thank you," he told her when she had finished. He drew himself up and took a deep breath. There were rich pickings to be had. "Perhaps you'll let them know that I'm here."

Fourteen

By mid-morning it had begun to rain. The clouds
lowered, the tops of the mountains disappeared.
None of the Bagthorpes had been pursuing outdoor
activities since their arrival, but now they realized that
they urgently wished to. The rain was of an impress-
ive order; puddles formed in the drive almost visibly.
(They were also forming elsewhere, as the Bagthorpes
would soon discover.)

"I said it'd rain," Mrs Fosdyke said, more or less to
herself, as she rattled about on her formica table. "I
said all along it'd rain. It'll be on for a week, likely,
now it's started."

"Never mind," said Mrs Bagthorpe brightly. "We
all have plenty to do."

"Like what?" demanded William. "This lot'll
interfere with my signals. They're crackling like hell
as it is."

"We – we must pretend that we are in the Victorian
era," said his mother. "We must provide our own
pastimes and entertainments."

"Like what?" said William again.

"Like – like charades," she said.

"At eleven o'clock in the morning?" inquired Mr
Bagthorpe. "Are you mad?"

His wife racked her brains desperately.

"The Victorians collected things," she said. "Fossils, and – and seashells, and arranged and catalogued them on wet days."

"And where, in the name of all that is wonderful, are we to collect those things at this moment?" he asked. "Pull yourself together, Laura. We are fifty miles from the sea."

"We must all use our ingenuity," she replied, undaunted by this undeniable truth. "The Victorians were quite Self Sufficient, and so must *we* learn to be."

"I thought we'd been through all that," William said.

"I don't mean Self Sufficient in the *literal* sense," she said. "I mean that we must rely upon our own inner resources."

"I, of course, have always been sufficient unto myself," Grandma remarked. "And my resources are considerable."

No one bothered to contradict her.

As the hours passed and the rain, far from clearing, became heavier, the atmosphere in Ty Cilion Duon became increasingly charged. There was not even the prospect of appetizing meals to look forward to.

"It'll be salad for lunch," Mrs Fosdyke announced. "Lettuce, and that corned beef out a tin."

"Why is that, Mrs Fosdyke?" asked her employer, knowing the effect this menu would have upon her family.

"There's no barbican going to work in that –" Mrs Fosdyke waved a soapy hand towards the window, streaming with water. "And no camping stove, neither."

"I could set up the stove in the outside—er, the outhouse," Jack offered, deliberately not specifying the nature of that building. It seemed, however, that she had now discovered this for herself. As he went out, he heard her say, "*I* ain't cooking in no toilet."

As it happened, the matter did not arise. The roof of the privy was leaking.

"There you are!" said Mrs Fosdyke. "It'll keep up for weeks, this rain, I shouldn't wonder."

She downed tools and went off to play dominoes with Grandpa. This maddened Mr Bagthorpe.

"Stop her!" he hissed to his wife. "I'm paying that Medusa wages, for God's sake!"

"Certainly not!" she hissed back. "Mrs Fosdyke is here on—well, on a kind of holiday, as the rest of us are."

At this stage Grandma started another record, and whispering became unnecessary. Mr Bagthorpe launched into a long and bitter monologue. He was hemmed in, he said, both by the mountains and by his own family. He found the mountains oppressive, they weighed upon his spirit, he despaired of writing a single line. Now, he was hemmed in by the rain. It was the last straw.

What was really needling him was being cut off from his favourite ally and weapon—the telephone. Withdrawal symptoms had set in almost from the moment of arrival, and were now becoming acute. Through the streaming windows he could make out the blurred shapes of the sheep, still safely grazing in the garden. What the hell, he wondered, was happening out there? Where were Mr Jones and his gun? Was Russell shot by now? If not—where was he? It seemed

185

an age since they had had a good slanging match over the telephone.

His frustration built up to a point when he finally jumped into the car and drove off down to the village, ostensibly to buy provisions, but really to find out what was going on. He drew a blank. When he entered The Welsh Harp he was met by stares of open hostility. He affected not to notice these, breezed up to the bar and shouted "Shop!" When he was finally served he made what he imagined to be jocular remarks about the beer being watered down, and asked the barman whether he thought the rain would keep up for a month, or merely a fortnight, and told him not to cut too many sandwiches.

"You can forget the passing trade, with this lot coming down," he said. "Ha!"

Seeing that his chance of wooing the natives was remote, his control snapped, and he pitched into them, instead.

"I've met two Welshmen so far today," he said to the saloon bar at large, "both called Jones. Very clever, when you come to think of it. I should think tax evasion is a doddle around these parts. *Any* kind of evasion. You might as well call yourself Anon, while you're at it."

There was silence, but for the heavy splatter of Welsh rain.

"Hands up if your name's Jones?" He suggested.

Blankness.

"You've probably all got the wrong mothers," he went on, warming to his theme. "You were probably all mixed up in the hospitals where you were born." He drained his glass, in case of the need for a quick getaway. "You are also probably all buried in the wrong graves, and under the wrong headstones."

The occupants of the bar remained impassive. Mr Bagthorpe was used to getting plenty of reaction, and now began to wonder if he was losing his touch.

"What do you do with the cards, at Christmas?" he asked. "Put 'em all in a heap, and shuffle them? What does it cost you a year in wrong numbers? How do you ever get *famous*, for God's sake?"

He had to raise his voice as he fired off these last shots because, at a nod from an old Jones in the inglenook, everybody now started talking. Mr Bagthorpe paused, triumphant. Now a real slanging match could begin.

He did not harbour this illusion for long. His audience were talking, all right, but to one another. And in Welsh.

Mr Bagthorpe cursed under his breath and headed for the door. As he emerged into the downpour he nearly tripped over a crowd of local boys, and cursed again. They sniggered and jeered as he wrenched open the door of the car. He drove off in a shower of spray and at a speed that would have done credit to Uncle Parker himself. As he made the right turn at the top of the village he glimpsed a blur of red shooting across his bows. He had missed his adversary by seconds, he realized, but did not turn round and follow him. It was beneath his dignity.

When he got back to base it was to find everyone running hither and thither with saucepans and buckets, and shouting. The Bagthorpes had discovered the leaks. Ty Cilion Duon now had not only Black Corners, it had wet ones as well.

187

"Quick, Father!" Rosie shrieked. "Come and help! It's pouring upstairs!"

"Oh *there* you are, Henry!" cried Mrs Bagthorpe. "Give me the car keys—I must buy more buckets!"

She snatched them from him and shot out. Mr Bagthorpe went into his study and slammed the door. Almost immediately there was a banging.

"There's your dinner 'ere!" shouted Mrs Fosdyke. "I'll put it down. I'm not 'aving that littering my kitchen till tea-time!"

There came the sound of crockery and cutlery clattering on the flagstones. Mr Bagthorpe waited a few minutes, then inched open the door. He snatched up the plate and bowl and retreated again. He put the dishes on his formica desk and eyed them. He hated salads at the best of times, believing that they were fit only for rabbits. He pushed this one aside and listlessly raised a spoonful of what looked like quite a promising trifle to his lips. He instantly spat it back into the dish. The overpowering fumes of garlic had even, it seemed, got into the custard.

He collapsed into his deckchair and buried his head in his hands. He remained like this for a long time.

Mr Bagthorpe often *acted* as if he were cornered and desperate. Now, he actually was.

"Why," he wondered, "did I ever come here? Why did I believe it would stimulate my creativity? Why could my holiday home not be like other people's, with carpets and telephones? Why cannot I make contact with the Other Side?"

There seemed to be no answers to any of these questions. Raising his head for a moment, he encountered the gaze of a wet sheep, its face pushed up

against the window-pane. He grabbed the nearest object to hand and hurled it. Both beer bottle and window smashed, and the sheep fled. The relentless Welsh rain now pattered steadily on the floor and sill. He sat and watched it dully.

The idea was vaguely forming in his mind that he must get out of Wales, or go mad. He numbly realized that he did not now care whether or not he did see a ghost. The only trouble was, that he had many times proclaimed that he would not budge from Ty Cilion Duon until he had. To leave now, without a single sighting, without even a sniff at a spectre, would be to suffer a crippling loss of face.

"There must be a way," he told himself, with a rare attempt at Positive Thinking.

The obvious way was to kill himself. He toyed with this idea for a time but it did not, on the whole, attract him. He felt that it was the wrong time of year.

"We're right in the middle of the silly season," he reflected. "And I wouldn't get proper obituaries and media coverage. You have to cross the Atlantic on a billiard table to get in the news."

He thought of pretending to have pneumonia on account of the damp, but was frightened that he might overdo it and end up in hospital (especially a Welsh one). He thought of ringing a friend, and asking him to ring back with the news that Mr Bagthorpe was urgently needed at Television Centre, and would have to be on standby for the next six weeks. The snags were that in the first place Mr Bagthorpe did not have a single friend in the world (not at any rate of the kind prepared to lie on his behalf) and in the second, of course, there was no telephone.

"I really am in hell here," he thought. "I don't deserve it. I owe it to myself to get myself out."

When he finally did come up with an idea it seemed to him a good one, but expensive. Mr Bagthorpe was not as mean as Grandma made him out to be (she said that he would cadge the last light off the Little Match Girl) but he was mean. His scheme would involve bribery on quite a large scale. He moodily weighed the pros and cons. He was already massively out of pocket from having paid the rent of Ty Cilion Duon in advance, and buying wardrobes and antlers. On the other hand, he seriously thought it possible that if he stopped in Wales he might never write another word. This was what really swung it.

"I owe it to my public," he told himself. "I owe it to the world."

He fished out his wallet and carefully counted out its contents. This exercise was a painful one, but at the same time he felt a curious lightening of the heart.

"This time tomorrow, we could be on our way out of Wales," he thought, and a picture of Unicorn House, bathed in a rosy glow, floated into his head.

During the time Mr Bagthorpe was in his study hatching up his plans, activities on the other side of the door had become increasingly hectic and noisy. The Vienna State Opera Choir were running a poor second. He now, for the first time, noticed this.

He flung open the door, and tripped straight over a sodden sheep. As he yelped and went headlong, he felt a sharp pain at the back of his neck. He clutched at it and felt teeth sink into the flesh of his hand. He struggled to his knees. Little Tommy crouched hissing and spitting on his left shoulder like Long John Silver's parrot. Before his dazed eyes passed what looked like an endless stream of sheep. They had evidently found their leader, who had decided that the way home lay through the back door of Ty Cilion Duon and out of the front.

It would not have been so bad if they had stuck to this itinerary. Sheep, however, are notoriously bad marchers in line. They wander off at tangents and round in circles.

When the leader trotted in at the kitchen door it could not have known that the route through the hall was blocked by scattered mounds of the Bagthorpes' belongings. It came up against these obstacles, and halted. The rest of the sheep must then have assumed that they had already arrived at their destination, and set about investigating their new pastures. Some went into the sitting-room, others attempted the stairs and several ran back into the kitchen.

As Mr Bagthorpe tried desperately to loosen the claws of Thomas the Second, Mrs Fosdyke came hell-for-leather out of the kitchen, screaming and brandishing the frying pan. As she passed him, making for the stairs, the cat made a leap, and next moment was crouched on *her* shoulder. The screech she emitted was of the order that shatters wine glasses.

Mr Bagthorpe, trying to clutch both his hand and his neck, looked wildly about him.

"Get them out of here!" he yelled. "Where's the bloody shepherd?"

He went unheard. Possibly never before in the Bagthorpe Saga had so many decibels been competing in such a confined space. It was the sheep that did it. As Mr Bagthorpe later remarked, the odd distant bleat in the meadows all of an April evening was one thing, but get a whole flock in a frenzy under one roof, and you have another can of worms entirely.

"It was like the Hallelujah Chorus," he declared, "sung in Greek for the Eurovision Song Contest."

He also maintained that the sheep had blown their minds on account of inhaling garlic fumes, and blamed Mrs Fosdyke for the whole thing.

192

Several teenage boys now appeared and started running here and there, shouting instructions at the sheep. They shouted these in Welsh, which meant that none of the Bagthorpes could understand them. Unfortunately, nor did the sheep seem able to.

Jack, hoping that Zero might make a name for himself as a sheepdog, set him among the flock. But all he did was imitate them. He ran hither and thither looking as lost and hopeless as any of the sheep and would, one felt, have bleated had he known how.

At this stage Uncle Parker appeared, as so often he did at the Bagthorpes' most hideous moments. He, unlike anyone else present, stood perfectly still, taking in the scene, an amused smile playing on his lips.

"All we need now's Daisy and the goat," Jack thought. "Oh help – they're here!"

Daisy came jostling through the sheep with Billy Goat Gruff in tow, looking none the worse for his spell in police custody. He looked, indeed, uncommonly snazzy, with his full complement of bells, plus brand new orange ribbons and a new trim of tassels.

"I *tol'* you d'ey'd come home!" shrieked that unholy child. "Dey all comed home, bringing their tails behind dem!"

This seemed to Jack a poor summary of the situation. He could not remember the nursery rhyme saying anything about hell. He started to push his own way towards Uncle Parker and reached him just as Mrs Bagthorpe returned.

She stood there, dangling multicoloured plastic buckets, eyes popping.

"Give me those keys!" yelled her husband. He snatched them from her and bolted. He had gone to execute his plan for flight from Wales, and to hell with the expense.

Nobody knew this, of course. It seemed likely to Jack, having glimpsed his father's expression, that he had gone to throw himself off a Welsh mountain.

Fifteen

By evening the sheep had gone. Ty Cilion Duon
looked – and smelled – like a farmyard. It looked as if
a million sheep had run loose in it.

How they had eventually been rounded up and
driven off no one was sure. Certainly the boys who
had run around waving sticks and uttering strange
Welsh cries did not seem to have helped. Mr
Bagthorpe had departed like a rat off a sinking ship,
and Mrs Fosdyke had gone upstairs, put her hat on,
and gone into another trance. Mrs Bagthorpe was
much alarmed by this. Somehow, this trance seemed
more serious than the previous ones, in which Mrs
Fosdyke had been bareheaded. The hat seemed to
stand for something.

The scene in the bedroom where she sat was quite
surrealistic. There were only the beds to sit on, and
Mrs Fosdyke, Grandma and Grandpa all sat there,
together (the other bedrooms had sheep in them) yet
strangely isolated, one entranced, one Breathing and
the third playing Solitaire. All about them the rain
came down in heavy, irregular spatters.

When the last of the sheep had scampered out of
the front door, writing off yet another tennis racket as

it left, the house went suddenly and eerily silent. The
only sound was that of the rain, inexorably filling
buckets and saucepans and flowing over.

Mrs Bagthorpe pushed her tumbled hair from her
eyes and staggered wearily through the mud towards
the kitchen. Jack followed, and watched her fill the
kettle from the single rusted tap.

"Tea," he heard her murmur. "Hot, sweet tea."

Gone was the Mills and Boon heroine of the
morning. She had come back to earth with a thump.
Jack thought her belief in the restorative power of hot
sweet tea touching.

"Not all the hot sweet tea in Arabia," he thought
confusedly, "is going to sweeten this little lot."

The Bagthorpes were as ones shell-shocked. It was
very dark outside, but no one bothered to turn on the
lights. For quite a long time after the sheep had left
they just sat there, drinking tea, numb and dumb.

When Grandma came down she immediately put
on another aria. One of the few things the sheep had
failed to destroy was her gramophone. The records,
however, were more seriously damaged than ever,
and the music was correspondingly fractured.

She then entered the kitchen. The silence in there
soon got on her nerves.

"There is one thing," she remarked. "Our resources have certainly been as stretched today as those of any Victorians."

Nobody bothered to reply. She made one or two more attempts to stir things, then gave up. It seemed to Jack that even she, despite her game attempts to start a good Row, looked weary, with violet shadows about her eyes. Even she now appeared vulnerable and mortal.

Mr Bagthorpe appeared, having been missing throughout the rounding up of the sheep. No one even troubled to look up, except Grandma. The silence soon got on his nerves, too.

"What's the matter with you lot?" he asked. "Sheep got your tongue? Ha!"

Mrs Fosdyke came in, still wearing her hat and, incongruously, her pinny and fur-edged slippers. She walked blindly over to the kettle and filled it. To Jack's surprise she carried it over to the camping stove and put it on. She made no comment about this potentially explosive article being in her kitchen. It was possible that she no longer cared if she *were* blown up.

The Silence was all at once broken by Mrs Bagthorpe.

"We must leave in the morning, Henry," she said. "We must leave this place tomorrow."

The words came out very slow, and measured, as if they had been long ruminated.

"Nonsense, Laura," said Mr Bagthorpe. "Where is your fighting spirit?"

"Gone," she replied simply. She sounded the least Positive Jack had ever heard her, even after the Fires.

197

"Jack, dear, go and put another record on," Grandma requested. She had perked up somewhat at the sight of her son, who could be relied on not to sit staring into space for long.

"You stop where you are," Mr Bagthorpe told him. "Where's Russell?"

"Gone," Jack said. "Went ages ago. He said he was allergic to sheep, except in fields."

"Typical," said Mr Bagthorpe, who was a fine one to talk. "Cares for nothing but his own comfort."

Certainly no one could have accused the Bagthorpes of this. They sat hunched in their smelly and devastated kitchen, the rain falling about them sporadically. Before them lay what promised to be the longest night of their lives. No one knew whether there were any beds dry enough to sleep in. No one even knew for sure that there was not still the odd sheep *under* the beds.

Secretly, however, some of them were resolved that this would be their last night at Ty Cilion Duon – notably Mr Bagthorpe, who had laid careful plans. Tess and William had each, unknown to the other, decided to spend their own pocket-money on rail tickets back to England. Rosie intended to go up the castle in the morning, and beg to be allowed to stay there with Daisy and Billy. Mrs Fosdyke's own plans were foggy, but had something to do with hoped-for hospitality from her new friends in The Welsh Harp.

Given this, no one even suggested clearing up. The task seemed hopeless, anyway. On this occasion, they really were in something resembling the Augean stables.

"Who's for a séance, then?" asked Mr Bagthorpe.

In the distance came the first faint rumblings of thunder.

"Oh don't, don't!" Rosie half-sobbed.

Mrs Bagthorpe got up.

"I will take the car and go and fetch fish and chips for supper," she announced. "Mrs Fosdyke cannot possibly be expected to cater under such conditions."

Mrs Fosdyke showed no signs of catering anyway. She showed no signs of listening, even.

"While I am gone," Mrs Bagthorpe continued, "you can all set about collecting your things, ready for departure tomorrow."

"We are not leaving this place until I have seen a ghost," her husband said.

"Then you can stay on alone, Henry," she told him. "Now – who's plaice, and who's cod?"

By nine o'clock the Bagthorpes' makeshift supper had been consumed and they were all bone-weary. They wanted to get to their beds, however wet.

"It may well be that the wardrobe is the driest place," Mr Bagthorpe said. "I may well kip down there myself – or in the boiler – ha!"

They climbed the stairs, or went to their ground floor billets, seeking oblivion. Thunder rumbled in the surrounding Welsh mountains.

"Don't all lie awake counting sheep!" Mr Bagthorpe shouted after them.

He had uncharacteristically volunteered to stay up last and check the lights and doors, a job that his wife did not really trust him to do, but didn't care, anyway.

Mrs Bagthorpe had once told Jack that the power of Positive Thinking was such that even if you were freezing cold, if you *told* yourself that you were warm, you would *feel* warm. He lay for quite a long while testing this theory by telling himself that his sleeping bag was really dry.

"It doesn't work," he decided. Just before he fell asleep he saw the flicker of lightning through his closed eyelids and heard a crack of thunder.

"If there are any ghosts in the Black Corners, this should fetch them out," was his last waking thought.

When he next woke he could not think for a moment where he was or what was happening. But he had the definite impression that he had been woken *by* something – or someone. He pulled himself up to a sitting position. As he did so, there was a prolonged, brilliant flare of lightning. In it he saw, standing in the sitting-room doorway, a motionless figure, draped in white from head to foot. At the same time he heard Zero give a low growl – or snore.

The blackness following the lightning was intense. Jack strained into it, his heart pounding. He could make out nothing at all.

"At least it doesn't g-g-glow," he thought.

He was terrified. He had forgotten all about seeing

Zero's fur stand up on end. He tried to remember whereabouts in the room William had finally kipped down. It was a large room. Nevertheless Jack began, very cautiously, to shuffle out of his bag. Then, stealthily, he began to crawl on his hands and knees.

"I hope I'm not heading towards the d-d-doorway," he thought.

His groping hand encountered something soft. He jumped violently and rose to his knees. There was another flash. Jack saw that the doorway was now empty. This was no comfort.

"N-now where's it g-g-gone?" he wondered. It could now jump out at him from any direction.

He still did not know where William was. Even when he did locate him, there was no guarantee that he could manage to waken him. William was a very heavy sleeper. Alarm clocks regularly failed to get through to him and would do so, Mr Bagthorpe said, until someone came up with one that sounded the Last Trump.

Jack decided that as the only bearing he was sure of was that of the doorway, which now seemed vacant, his best course would be to make for the light switch. He remembered Mrs Fosdyke's lugubrious pronouncement: "There's only the light'll drive out the Powers of Darkness."

This he did, getting his knees decidedly wet in the process. With tremendous relief he found the door jamb, pulled himself to his feet and found the switch. He pressed it. Nothing happened. He groaned.

As he stood there, it suddenly seemed not quite so dark.

"Dawn!" he thought. "Thank heaven!"

Dawn, however, did not usually flicker. Jack turned towards the hall and saw, half-way up (or down) the stairs, a wavering candle-flame.

"The B-b-b-bearded M-m-man C-c-carrying a C-c-candle!"

Jack wished that he could faint. He tried to, shutting his eyes in the effort. When he opened them again, the candle was bobbing somewhere on the landing above. He found himself unable to scream or yell. He thought it might attract attention to himself. He blundered about, tripping over rackets and stags' antlers, groping for another switch. Almost sobbing with relief he found one and again pressed it. Nothing.

By now, someone else seemed to be sobbing.

"Oh lummee!" he thought, "The Small Child W-w-weeping! Oh help!"

All the Black Corners of Ty Cilion Duon, it seemed, were disgorging their ghastly inmates at once. Jack made another determined effort to faint.

"Where's that dog?" he found himself thinking. "Where's that mutton-headed hound?"

There was another flash of lightning. Jack had the horrified impression that he now saw *two* Veiled Ladies, one by the kitchen door, the other half-way up (or down) the stairs.

"I expect they'll find me in the morning, foaming at the mouth and with my hair turned snow-white from shock," Jack thought. He did not feel that he could stand much more.

As it happened, he did not have to. From the landing above there came an almighty crash, then an instant's silence, followed by a babble of voices.

"Help, help!" Jack yelped, the spell broken. "Quick – Zero – William – Mother – help!"

From upstairs came screams and shrieks louder even than his own. In his confused state it seemed to him that most of the voices were unfamiliar, but they didn't sound like those of ghosts. What the clamour reminded him of, more than anything, was the school playground, at break. There certainly seemed to be quite a lot of bad language mixed in with it.

Then, above it all, Jack heard Mr Bagthorpe's unmistakable yell.

"Hell fire! What's going on?"

"Daddy Daddy Daddy!" came Rosie's gabble, in a tone going right back to nursery days. "Oh please oh please I'm scared!"

"Clear off, you loon!"

"*I'm* the Veiled Lady, you dumbo!"

"I'll get you for this!"

"Oooh – me garlic – where's me garlic?"

At least Jack recognized the last of these voices.

"Fozzy!" he yelled. "Oh, quick!"

He had not thought to live to see the day when he would be enraptured to hear Mrs Fosdyke's voice.

The confusion that followed was unique in the Bagthorpe Saga. To Jack, it seemed as if not only all the Black Corners were erupting at once, but that some kind of World Boxing Championship was being held as well. As he cowered against the wall by the defunct light-switch, he glimpsed, in the intermittent flares of lightning, hand to hand fighting going on all over the place. The row was tremendous. In the end, even William woke up.

Without warning, the place was flooded with light.

203

Jack put his arm over his eyes, convinced that his end was near. Then, amazingly, a hush descended. Slowly he raised his head.

There, frozen in tableau by the sudden light, he saw six, seven, eight—more, even, figures scattered about the hall and stairway, none of them being members of the family, and none of them looking particularly like apparitions.

"Hell's bells!"

Jack saw his father fling open the door of the kitchen (where, it later appeared, he had been stationed by the switch of the main electricity supply).

"Give me my money back!" he yelled obscurely. "You've fouled it up, the lot of you!"

A further commotion set up. One by one bleary-eyed members of the family congregated while the interlopers, unnoticed, made their getaway.

"Who *were* all those people?" cried Mrs Bagthorpe, as they assembled, more or less automatically, in the kitchen for the Inquest. "They were children, surely? Juveniles?"

"Oh, is it tomorrow yet?" sobbed Rosie. "Are we going home?"

They were. The final Inquest on the Night of the Black Corners was not held until the Bagthorpes were back at Unicorn House and the Parkers at the Knoll.

What had happened was a kind of unwitting overkill—Mr Bagthorpe and Uncle Parker having both had more or less the same idea. The former was keen to get out of Ty Cilion Duon at any price, the latter being threatened by the sheep-farmer and his gun, and afraid that the Welsh police were out to get

204

him. The only way escape seemed possible was if a ghost, or ghosts, was sighted. Mr Bagthorpe had categorically stated that he would not stir until this happened, and Daisy Parker was refusing point blank to go home until the Bagthorpes did.

"They my bes' friends in the world," she had kept telling her father, who was only too well aware that the converse was certainly not the case.

Uncle Parker and Mr Bagthorpe had each quite independently hit upon the idea of having certain of the local youth impersonate the phantoms described by Mr Jones as being in more or less permanent residence.

Mr Bagthorpe refused to concede that this was a case of great minds thinking alike.

"Do not classify my mind with his," he said. "You might as well classify Plato with Mickey Mouse."

It turned out that the boys who had run round the house after the sheep were on Uncle Parker's payroll, and were getting the lie of the land in preparation for their hauntings, later. Mr Bagthorpe's gang had not been so well briefed. And neither gang, of course, was aware of the other's existence – to begin with, at least.

With there being two of everything – two Veiled Ladies, two Small Children Weeping etcetera, it was inevitable that eventually wires would become crossed. It ended up with the haunters haunted.

Both Bearded Men Carrying Candles dropped them, and it was lucky that the house was so thoroughly soaked, or there would inevitably have been a fire beyond Daisy Parker's wildest dreams.

The stay in Wales cost Mr Bagthorpe dear. His only consolation was that Uncle Parker's bill for the destruction caused by Daisy's activities as Bo Peep was probably even larger than his own. Uncle Parker hugged to himself the secret knowledge of the identity of the absentee landlord of Ty Cilion Duon. It was the Mr Jones whose goat had been winged by mistake, and who had later dined with the Parkers at the castle. He intended to reveal this information to Mr Bagthorpe during a Row at some later date, when it was too late for him to act upon it.

It is hideously embarrassing to come back early from a holiday. Most people stick it out to the bitter end, take plenty of photographs and spend the rest of the year talking about how marvellous it was. This kind of pretence is virtually impossible when you have booked for six weeks, and are back within the week. The family could have hatched up some plausible story to explain their early return, but they had, as Mr Bagthorpe said "an everlasting fly in the gravy".

Mrs Fosdyke had a field day in The Fiddler's Arms. She made Ty Cilion Duon sound even worse than it was, decorating it up with cockroaches, death-watch beetles and Welsh rats (which were, she maintained, twice as big as English ones and with twice as many teeth).

The Bagthorpes plunged frenziedly back into what was, for them, everyday life, and tried hard to blot out all memory of their ill-fated venture Abroad. The only happy memory they had was that of the destruction of the wardrobe. Mr Bagthorpe refused to pay for its removal to Unicorn House, but had no intention of bequeathing it to the absentee Mr Jones.

"If we do," he told everybody, "he'll be advertising it as a self-contained holiday chalet, and letting it at a hundred quid a week."

He wanted to set fire to it, but was prevented by the persistent downpour. He then proposed ringing The National Trust, to see if they wanted to take it on. But in the end he simply took an axe and smashed it.

Rosie took a photograph of this and it came out well, despite the rain. She then blew it up and framed it and hung it in the downstairs loo, where for a long time to come the Bagthorpes were to sit and ponder on the undeniable drawbacks of Abroad.